Kings of Paradise

Award Winning Author

MAXINE DOUGLAS

Rings of Paradise © 2012 by Maxine Douglas

All rights reserved. No part of this book may be reproduced or transmitted in any form or by any means, electronic or mechanical, including photocopying, recording, or by any information storage and retrieval system, without permission in writing from the publisher.
The characters and events portrayed in this book are fictitious. Any similarity to real persons, living or dead, or events, is coincidental and not intended by the author.
This book was written by a human and not Artificial Intelligence (A.I.).
This book cannot be used to train Artificial Intelligence (A.I.).

Print Edition

Cover Art © 2024 by D.H. Fritter (via BookBrush)

Previously published by:
The Perfect Match, Whiskey Creek Press, 2005
The Perfect Match, Class Act Books, 2008
MuseItUp Publishing, 2012

Books by Maxine Douglas

Widows of Blessings Valley Series
Elizabeth
Vera

Men of the Double K Series
Red River Crossing
Winds of Change
Game of Chance (2025)

Brides Along the Chisholm Trail Series
The Reluctant Bride
The Marshal's Bride
The Cattleman's Bride

Nashville Duets Series
Nashville Rising Star
Nashville by Morning

American Historical / Gilded Age Romance
Deceitful Promises (2024/2025)
Hannah's Discovery (Reclusive Man Series)
Victoria (Book 19, Angel Creek Christmas Brides)
Leanna's Light (Book 12, Alphabet Mail-Order Brides)

Contemporary Romance / Romantic Suspense
Simply to Die For (2025 re-release)
The Gingerbread Inn (Christmas at the Inn Series)
Road Angel
Knight to Remember
Rings of Paradise
Blood Ties

YA Cozy Mystery
Reading, Writing and Catmetic (Holiday Pet Sleuth Mysteries)

DEDICATION

For my father who never missed a single televised bout,
and went to as many live ones as he could.
Always remember "Fishing's fake, wrestling's real!"

PRAISE FOR

Rings of Paradise

"RINGS OF PARADISE is an awesome read and I will tell my friends all about it!!!"
by Racegirl

"The unique plot and the great characters kept me turning the pages of this contemporary romance."
by Cheryl C. Malandrinos

"…the story was really good that I cannot give it a lower rating than a 5."
by SmallMallReads

"RINGS OF PARADISE is a superbly told, sexy romance. I'll be looking for more books by Maxine Douglas soon."
by The Book Connection

ACKNOWLEDGMENTS

Thank you to the men and women who play at this game so many of us enjoy. And to those who have fallen, we miss you.

Thank you for any inspiration provided by:
Van Halen, Journey, David Lee Roth
Los Angeles Dodgers
Madison Metro
Miami Vice

PROLOGUE

Shadoe Donovan stood in front of the large office window overlooking the bay of Lake Monona. His six-foot, two-inch muscular frame cast a shadow over the thirty-something man sitting behind a weathered oak desk.

"When did all this happen?" The man's voice came from behind him.

"Officially, the deal was signed last night." Shadoe smiled, feeling a bit of pity for the man. *Hell, if someone suddenly walked in off the street telling me he'd just bought the company I worked years for, I'd be a bit pissed off, as well.*

"Why this magazine?"

"It's small, virtually unknown...exactly what I was looking for." Watching the local ski team practice their routine to perfection, he felt their aches and pains as they worked to hone each move with precision. He felt his own aching muscles spasm in response.

"For what? A tax write-off after you've driven it further into the ground?" The voice came again, edged with sarcasm and irritation.

"Look here, Scott—"

"My name is Ric, damn it!"

Shadoe turned from the window as one of the skiers completed a jump. "Right now, all I'm looking for is someone to write a story. I want a fresh, unbiased unknown for this. Someone with the drive and desire to tell the truth as they see it, who's not afraid of a little bit of controversy."

"Controversy?" Ric Scott turned away from the files he'd been asked to get. "Just what the hell is this story about, anyway?"

Shadoe observed the man a bit closer. Ric Scott was going to be just the person he needed to keep things under control while he was away on other business. He had a reputation for being dynamic in his profession. So far, everything Shadoe had heard about the editor-in-chief was right on the money, including the shooting-straight-from-the-hip warning.

"Pro wrestling." Shadoe smiled, watching closely for the normal reaction to the game he loved so much, a profession many people considered a circus of highly paid performers. He supposed they could be right about the circus part. In the past few years, he'd been asked to wear costumes his father wouldn't have put on for any amount of money.

"Are you nuts? Controversy is right." Tossing down a pencil, Ric pushed away from his desk.

"I'll be damned if I'll let you bring this magazine down with that kind of cover-up story," he continued. "We write the truth, not some sugar-coated soap! Our readers aren't a bunch of hicks; they're intelligent, well-educated members of society."

"Take it easy, Scott." Shadoe walked to the front of the desk. "I'm not about to change the format. I just want a writer to do this exposé, is all."

Standing over the man, Shadoe knew under usual circumstances his size and attitude could be intimidating, but this wasn't the case here. Even at a less imposing five-foot-eight, Ric Scott wasn't about to back down from him, and he liked that fact very much.

"I have a plane to catch. I don't have time to pull rank with you. Let's see who's on staff and go from there." Shadoe pulled up one of the large winged-back leather chairs.

Shadoe listened to Ric as he read each staff member's credentials. Sitting back in the chair, he knew halfway through the files not one of the staff would fit what he was looking for.

"Look, Scott," he began, sitting forward. "Everyone so far has experience. If the rest of them do, too, I can't use them for this assignment."

"All right, Donovan, just why do you want a virtual unknown?" Scott sighed. "Unless you're ready for a lawsuit, which, by the way, would destroy the magazine, an experienced journalist would be best."

"As for the legal and financial condition of this magazine, it's of no concern to you." Shadoe liked the directness and aggression of Scott. The fact that this man was so protective of the magazine and its staff was a welcome relief, but he wasn't about to play nursemaid to the man.

"This company can handle anything thrown at it from now on. As for the why, it's time for the fans to know how hard pro wrestlers train every day of the year, how difficult it is on their families when they're on the road ninety percent of the time," he continued, walking back over to the window, gazing at the lake and the lone boater drifting out on the water. He felt much of his life was like that boat, just going with the flow, never really coming to rest for a long time.

"Besides, I'm the boss, and I said so." Returning to the desk, he once again stood with authority over Scott. "Because it's the sport that's enabled me to follow the career I love and cherish more than anything or anyone. I owe it to the wrestlers who have been disabled for life or even given their life in the ring for the love of the game."

Shadoe watched the reasoning register deep in Scott's mind as he let him think. He glanced at his watch. His plane was due to leave in less than two hours. If things didn't progress right now, he'd never get through security and would miss his flight to Hawaii. The cocky posture diminished slightly with each passing moment until at last Scott exhaled in a small surrender.

"Okay, I get the picture. I may just have the person you're looking for." Scott ran his hands through his short, dark hair, hesitation flashing through his face.

"Great! Who is he?"

"It's not a he." Scott smirked. "It's a she.

There's no real formal training or experience. Just the drive and desire to write. Her name's Khristen Roberts, but she's on a long-deserved vacation."

"Perfect. Put her on the assignment as soon as you can reach her." Shadoe stepped toward the door. "I've got a plane to catch. I'll be in touch with the details soon."

"What's your connection, Donovan? What makes you think you've got the inside track to this 'secret' society?"

Shadoe turned just as he reached for the door. Pausing, he looked Ric Scott straight in the eye, deciding quickly to tell him just how connected he was.

"Ever hear of 'The Flame'?"

CHAPTER 1

Khristen Roberts cleared her throat. "Excuse me, but you're sitting in my seat."

"Oh?" The casually dressed man made no effort to move from the seat he boldly sprawled his body across. He sat as if he owned this entire section of the plane, especially the two seats he now occupied.

"Listen, if you want the window seat, that's just fine with me. There'll be nothing to see but water, anyway." Khristen Roberts forced a polite smile. She stood waiting for the man to remove his legs from the only empty set left in first class. She wasn't about to sit in coach. She'd worked too hard and too long for this vacation and particularly that seat.

Not even off the ground yet. Who does this guy think he is, anyway?

Perturbed, Khristen glimpsed her reflection in his mirrored glasses. Not only was the obnoxious, handsome man sitting in her seat, but his large legs swung over onto her now-inherited seat, as well.

Khristen took matters in her own hands and pushed the bare, hairy, tanned, muscular legs out of her way.

"What the—" The soft, deep voice rang out in surprise as he tore the sunglasses away from his eyes—eyes the color of clear seawater, brilliant and dangerous.

A woman could drown in eyes like that.

She felt herself slipping into their deep waters without a life jacket.

"What's going on here?"

Confusion and disbelief were very much evident in those sea-green eyes, as well as in his voice. Even the muscles in his biceps seemed to twitch with surprise. Or was it aggravation?

Serves him right.

"You, sir, are in my seat." Khristen fought to control the building irritation as she sat down. "I paid good money for it and don't intend to share it with you or your legs."

She snatched a magazine out from the back of the seat and flipped through it. Not really seeing the contents of each page, she wondered what lucky star she had wished on to be stuck next to this despicable hunk all the way to Hawaii. Despicable was the nicest word she could think of to describe him at the moment. He was the type who thought muscles and a nice body got him his way. She had dealt with his kind before. She'd successfully kicked each one to the gutter each and every time. Well, almost each and every time… but she wasn't going to dwell on that mistake.

Khristen ignored the confusion as the final passengers boarded the plane. She figured it would be ten minutes or so before they would even begin to taxi out onto the Los Angeles airport runway.

Khristen fastened her seat belt and prayed sleep would come for the remainder of her flight to her long-awaited tropical vacation. As soon as they were in the air, she would locate a station on the radio and let her mind tune in to some good, hard '80s rock music. Maybe some Van Halen, or Journey, or better yet, David Lee Roth, anything to make the four-hour trip go faster. She hoped it would keep her mind from wandering over to the guy who sat next to her—a man who smelled as good as he looked—all spice and dangerous as hell.

"You know, you were pretty rude." The deep, smooth-as-silk, masculine voice pierced the silence she'd tried to plant between them.

So much for solitude.

"Me!" The anger in her eyes reflected off the mirrored sunglasses on her unwelcome travel companion. "You should talk, Mister My-Future's-So-Bright-I–Gotta-Wear-Shades. I'm not the seat-stealer here." Khristen's nerves snapped with aggravation.

In a desperate attempt to calm down before her mouth got her thrown off the plane, Khristen rested her head against the back of her seat. She closed her eyes, hoping to put an end to the unwanted conversation. As entertaining as it may end up, she didn't want to tempt fate.

Been there and done that, as the saying goes, in

another place and time. No need to repeat the same mistake.

"That still doesn't give you the right—"

"Listen. It's going to be a long flight, and if you don't mind, I'd rather not spend my time bickering with you. You can have the seat, and let's just pretend that neither one of us is sitting next to the other. Okay? Okay," she said, clutching the magazine.

While the stewardess instructed them all on safety procedures, Khristen couldn't help notice her fellow traveler kept the silver-framed mirrored sunglasses perched on his nose. An unquenchable curiosity surged its way to the surface, causing an all-too-familiar feeling.

Damn hormones, anyway!

She felt them start their rampage through her body, and thoughts of the mysterious stranger mingled with a desire to figure out what he had to hide.

His body fueled her imagination as she tried to seek out his facial features—the ones she could see, anyway.

Daddy always warned me about being too curious. It only gets a girl going down the wrong path.

Too bad she hadn't taken those words to heart the last time she had taken a trip.

A little hidden inspection couldn't hurt, could it? Not if she was careful, and he didn't notice her giving him the once-over. She was only looking, not touching, after all. And he'd never know; if he fell asleep with those damn glasses on.

On his head sat a well-worn Los Angeles Dodgers baseball cap, covering curly, dark-brown hair that barely peeked out from under the brim. Khristen's gaze passed over his partially hidden face from the eyebrows to a somewhat crooked nose. His mouth seemed to carry a sense of seriousness at the corners of a pair of full lips—the kind that Khristen imagined could kiss a woman with fiery passion as easily as lash out a thousand whipping strokes.

A quick and unnerving surge passed through her body when her gaze followed the outline of his strong, squared jaw. With the plane ascending, her inspection rested at the end of his determined chin. A smile played across his lips.

"Like what you see?" His deep, silky voice challenged with a touch of conceit. Her eyes revealed everything she was feeling at that moment, if her mirrored reflection was true.

"Don't flatter yourself!" She was scarcely aware of her own voice or the warm glow touching her cheeks, but she was fully aware that he had messed up her ecosystem without as much as a touch.

He smiled fully, showing each and every pearl-white tooth. "Thanks, babe." He nonchalantly removed the baseball cap, the tucked-up hair spilling down around his shoulders.

Despite her obvious lame protest, she barely muffled the squeak of pleasure when her continued inspection took in the massive chest with the hair that peeked out the top of his black tank shirt. A mischievous smile threatened her lips as curiosity took hold of her again.

Mmmm, wonder where that leads?

She felt herself nearly reaching an uncontrollable level. Her warning bell should have been gonging a thousand times by now but wasn't.

Her body filled with natural female desire as Khristen focused on muscular tanned thighs hidden snugly in a pair of wild-colored spandex shorts. Her heart skipped a beat when his well-toned thigh muscle twitched.

A nervous sigh escaped her. She tried with all her might to subdue the unwanted longing and curiosity that could spell trouble.

Why do I always seem to go after a challenge?

She rested her head against the seat and tried in vain to suppress the smile crossing her face.

Because, that's what makes life interesting, and it's also what gets me in so much trouble.

Khristen pushed the thought of herself and the stranger out of her mind until restless sleep finally fell upon her.

* * * *

It was all Shadoe could do to keep from laughing. For the first time in years, here was a woman who didn't recognize him, or for that matter, even try to be civil toward him. He knew from the way her body pinked with embarrassment when she'd been checking him out that she was hot for him. Her gaze shot boiling lust over him and made him feel as if his clothing had melted from this body, leaving him naked and vulnerable.

The last thing he had expected from her was a flare-up. He had always gotten his way with women before.

Ha, maybe it was the women who got their way with me.

Rachel, his ex-wife, had been a prime example. Regardless, this woman was a regular spitfire.

It had been so long since he'd met a woman who did not crawl all over him that he was not sure what to do. Being a professional wrestler offered "companion" opportunities nightly; all he had to do was look around as he left an arena.

He longed for more than being on the road, and it gnawed at him more as the years passed. He'd watched his fellow wrestlers leave the business for one reason or another. One might say his biological clock was ticking.

He would have retired, quit the business years ago, before the deaths and injuries to some of his buddies woke him to the fact that the public needed to be educated about the game. He felt the only way to guarantee the truth was told to his satisfaction was to have it printed in his own magazine. He owed it to those fallen and to himself before it all ended for him.

Shadoe slipped off his glasses and listened to the even breathing from the woman beside him. Her breath gently raised her breasts. He wondered whether they were as firm as they appeared.

Good heavens, man, why can't they all be as challenging as this one? He wanted to trace the outline of her full lips with his fingertips, and he ached to calm the storm that had brewed between them moments ago. The feeling was unlike any he had ever experienced in his professional or personal life in quite a while.

Shadoe slid the glasses back on and turned to gaze out the window—her window—and wondered whether her hair felt as soft as the passing puffs of clouds looked.

* * * *

"Please return your trays to their upright..."

The words echoed softly in Khristen's mind, bringing her back through the sleepiness of the last three hours. Stretching to pull her cramped muscles from their stiffness, she opened her eyes and realized she'd fallen asleep with her head against her neighbor's shoulder.

"Well, she's back in the world, ready to grace me with her outstanding wit again."

"Sorry, forgot you were there." She set her seat in the upright position. "Out of sight, out of mind."

Who am I kidding? Maybe out of sight, but he firmly planted himself in my dream.

"Are you sure? That was a pretty sensual moan coming from you just before you stretched," he whispered, leaning toward her so close, she felt the warmth of his breath on her skin.

The sensual smirk on his face irritated her. He was ever more pompous than she'd first thought. "If it was, which I highly doubt…" She watched the Maui landscape come into view over his shoulder. "Rest assured the cause wasn't you."

"Or maybe you just didn't realize it was me," he said.

The plane's landing gear bumped the ground. "I think it was you dreaming, not me. After all, you're the one with the fixation on yourself."

"Maybe so, only I'm never alone in my dreams." The sharp and assessing look he gave her sent hot shivers down her spine.

What is it about this guy? Why do I even give him the time of day?

As the plane taxied into its arrival gate, their gazes met briefly, causing her blood to race through her veins. Heat flashed through her face, and she felt he had read her thoughts—wanton thoughts that surprised even her.

Khristen shook her head as if to put the marbles back in place. She reached into the overhead compartment for her overnight bag with him standing next to her as the plane taxied into the terminal.

"Let me get that for you." He placed his hand over hers.

"I'm perfectly capable of carrying one small piece of luggage." Her grip tightened under his.

She wasn't about to allow him to help her. She was perfectly capable of handling her own little overnight bag.

"At the moment, you don't look capable of doing anything but taking a cold shower." He tried to pull the bag from her as the plane jolted to a stop.

"Leave me." Khristen gave her bag one last tug, causing it to open and spilling the contents onto the floor of the plane.

"Now see what you've done!" She stooped to gather her overturned belongings as quickly as she could. Why couldn't he just leave her alone and let her get on with her life?

"Here, let me." Shadoe bent and picked up her

things and placed them in the bag, including her lacy panties and their matching bras. He held her undergarments between his thumb and forefinger for a moment. Dropping them, he picked up the nametag dangling outside the case in his hand.

"I can do it myself." Khristen grabbed and tossed the tag into the bag with the last of her things. She snapped the bag shut and headed for the departure door wondering what act of God had caused her case to fly open when it had been locked. She had a feeling this was going to be one hell of a vacation.

* * * *

"Khristen Roberts," Shadoe whispered to himself as he watched Khristen make her way to the back of the plane.

There couldn't be more than one of her, could there? She had snatched the ID tag fast, but he thought the city and state on it had read *Madison, Wisconsin*. He was still stunned by what he read. Was she his Khristen Roberts? Well, maybe not his but the magazine's?

It had to be her—the woman Ric Scott had recommended for the article that would most likely end his career. How many Madison, Wisconsin Khristen Roberts could there be in the world?

He hoped there was only one—the one who sparked something in him he once thought did not have a chance to ignite ever again; the one who for a few hours made him remember he was just a regular Joe, not the Universal Wrestling World Champion; the very one making her way down the little departure hallway. If he didn't follow suit, he'd lose her in the crowd.

He grabbed his athletic bag and followed her. If he lost her, he would either have to call all over Maui looking for her or contact Ric Scott to find out where Khristen Roberts from his newly acquired magazine was staying. As he saw it, his only option was the former.

CHAPTER 2

Wrapped in a large, fluffy, white towel, Khristen strolled around the hotel room that would be her home for the next two weeks. Two glorious weeks in paradise. Now that she was finally here, nothing would keep her from fulfilling her desire…and need…to take in all the island had to offer.

She slid open her balcony door a few inches, allowing the fresh, clean smell of the ocean to drift into the room. A hint of floral blossoms wafting through the screen reminded her of the beauty and simplicity of the beach.

Breathing deeply, she tossed the robe onto the unmade bed; the salty sea air sent refreshing shivers over her exposed skin. She couldn't wait to step outside and fill her being with the glorious sensation.

The morning was fully awake now, the view simply breathtaking. Below her, she watched the gentle swaying of palm trees on the golden sandy beach that stretched to the beautiful North Pacific Ocean. In the distance, the bright morning sun silhouetted the mountains on Lanai, giving them a halo of gold at their peaks.

A place for angels to rest their wings and find peace from the hectic human world.

Taken in by the beauty and quiet of the Hawaiian morning, she thought how busy her world back home would be right now. There was such a contrast between the two, this area serene and beautiful, the other hazy and noisy with cars full of people rushing off to work. She would be running around the office right now trying to get the next edition of the magazine ready.

Instead, she looked forward to having someone wait on her, even if it was the hotel staff performing their usual duties. She would definitely take this life of leisure over the one of confusion; at least until she needed something more to do than languish around on the beach.

She'd booked this vacation to take a long, hard look at her life. Over the past ten years, she had jumped from one job to another, never really feeling fulfilled by any of them. It was a chance meeting on the Madison Metro system one morning a few years ago that lead her to Ric Scott and *Plain Talk*.

Career-wise, she felt the path she was on to finally be the right one. She needed more after falling in love with the magazine business. She yearned to be more than Ric's copy editor. She wanted to be the one who wrote those monthly articles, who did the research and shared her findings with the readers.

Without a journalism degree, she knew the competition at the magazine would be tough. She needed to figure out how to convince Ric to let her try her hand at an article. The problem with this setting was that nothing but the beach occupied her mind, the plan to figure it out gone with the salty breeze.

She had lain in bed the night before for hours, contemplating a plan after unsuccessfully trying to recapture sleep. After several fitful hours, she had gotten out of bed. The ocean had called out to her. Before she realized it, she had thrown on a white cotton dress, slipped on a pair of beach sandals, and was strolling along the sandy shore in the wee morning hours of daybreak in hopes of capturing the joy of being alone to sort through her thoughts.

She hadn't been alone on the beach. A lone jogger had caught her slightly off guard as he trotted off in the distance on the sandy ground. She remembered thinking how familiar the man had appeared to be and then had quickly dismissed it when something in the sand caught her attention. As something now did.

The sun shining through the balcony door onto the dresser caught Khristen's attention. She stopped slipping on tennis shoes and followed the ray of light. She gazed at the spiral shell she had found earlier that morning in the sand and the once-fresh lei that had adorned her neck the day before. The floral scent no longer lingered in the air.

Much like life...here today, gone tomorrow.

* * * *

Khristen stepped out from the glass-enclosed elevator into the lobby, absent-mindedly letting her nose lead her hungry body to the aroma of breakfast being served in the dining room. After the hostess seated her at a small table, she scanned the menu, and then decided to stay with the usual: eggs over easy, hash browns, crisp bacon, and a large glass of orange juice. She may want to start being adventurous, but what she put in her stomach would remain the same. Predictable, familiar, and safe.

An animated conversation drew her attention to the hostess's station. There he stood in front of the woman. His shoulder-length brown hair, white shorts, and a tropical-print short-sleeved shirt accented his already tanned body. He turned and watched her mix her food. Her breath stopped like a quick electrical outage.

When their gazes met, a shock ran through her, caused by the warmth of his smile, and the gentle twinkling of those sea-green eyes. He winked broadly at her, causing yet another tremor of shyness to shoot right in her. Even from across the room, his gaze was piercing. She felt it prick at her heart, trying to penetrate the closed door.

Khristen looked away and continued to play with her food, her hunger forgotten. She peered up through her eyelashes to find him studying her.

The palms of her hands grew damp; a warm chill ignited her nerve ends. Could it be that he, too, was staying at the hotel?

There's no way it could be him. I don't think I could handle another vacation disaster in my life right now. Please, Cupid, point your arrow at another victim of love.

Then, he turned away and said something to the hostess and staff as if they were the only ones in the restaurant at eight o'clock in the morning. Their laughter hit a sour chord in the pit of her stomach for some unexplained reason. Jealousy? Over a man she didn't know? She wouldn't even consider that aspect at all. After all, she wasn't interested in getting to know him.

Or am I?

Khristen waited for him to leave before quickly signing her bill, charging it to her room, and moving with caution into the lobby. If she ran into him here, now, she'd end up embarrassing herself. So instead, she peeked around the corner and clung to the walls before stepping backward through the elevator doors. She let out the breath she hadn't realized she'd been holding, and relief flooded through her.

Safely back in her room, she sat on the edge of the bed and tried to collect her thoughts. Her fingers trembled as she fidgeted with the removal of her blouse, one button at a time. She didn't like the feelings that surged through her at the sight of an overly attractive man—especially that man. All that came to mind was Dane Harper and the pain he'd caused her after the last vacation she had taken.

She had gone to Branson, Missouri to check out some time-shares. Her vacation had been virtually paid for by the companies, except for her transportation and a few extra days spent at the hotel. It had been a way for her to take time from the magazine, see a new city, catch some of the shows, and enjoy the acts the popular tourist spot offered.

She'd accumulated a nice little nest egg over the years, so she would be able to buy if she liked what she saw, and the price was right. Just because she had the money didn't mean she'd jump on the first chance to blow it all at once.

She had been on one of the condo tours when she met Dane Harper. She'd been waiting in the small lobby with others when a six-foot, sandy-blond-haired man called out her name. He had introduced himself, and their tour began. They laughed and talked about their families and life in general. She'd felt a connection, and her romantic heart had flown into high gear and settled on her sleeve.

Officially, the sales pitch and tour had ended a few hours later, with her bank account still intact. Unofficially, the tour Dane had in mind had just begun.

He had convinced her that she shouldn't go to the shows or out on the town without an escort. He then offered to show her around and accompany her. Over the next three days, he'd called her in the morning and at noon and then shown up at her hotel in time to take her out for the night. She'd been swept off her feet for the first time by what her dad would have called a 'pretty boy.' Again, she should have listened to her father's advice.

She thought she had fallen in love.

She'd been falling all right—smack dab on her face. That had become all too clear when she ended up in bed alone, her car gone, and her pocketbook empty of all cash and credit cards.

Dane Harper was nowhere to be found, and the police found no evidence of his existence. They even went so far as to indicate that Dane Harper didn't exist except in her mind. The only one to believe her was Ric.

Dane had been smooth in every way—body as well as mind. He knew the game rules all too well and who to play them with. Khristen had sworn she would never trust another man with her heart.

When she had finally gotten back home, Ric had pulled in every marker to find the guy. Bottom line: Dane Harper had disappeared with more than half of her life savings and belongings. He had successfully stolen her heart, crushed it, and taught her that some promises did not hold an ounce of truth.

She may be tough on the outside, but inside, she prayed not all promises were meant to be broken. Somewhere, there was the right man for her. He may not be rich or gorgeous, but he would be honest and trustworthy.

She slipped into her canvas sandals and grabbed her cover-up, beach bag, and an oversized towel. A cool dip in the pool would clear her head of such nasty memories.

As she strolled with leisure along the manmade brick path through the courtyard and garden, a hummingbird fluttered among the many brightly-colored tropical flowers. The beauty of her surroundings made her forget any earlier frustrations.

Khristen continued the short trek to the pool

area and chose a chaise lounge she hoped would eventually be in the shade from the late afternoon sun. The white-lace cover-up slid off her shoulders. Khristen draped a towel over the woven material, positioned herself on the lounger, and then reached into the bag for a bottle of tanning oil.

* * * *

Shadoe came from the open-air Tiki Terrace and stood in the veil of the afternoon shadows. He watched every move Khristen made with intense interest. His eyes followed her delicate hand as she caressed shiny oil along her milky white shoulders. The hardness of desire and the hunger in his loins grew with each fluid movement as Khristen dripped more oil into her cupped hand and smoothed it along her shapely legs until they glistened in the bright sun.

When she had finally awakened from her nap, the look in those cool brown eyes of hers had dared him, and he found it hard to resist trying to unnerve the determination and confidence oozing from their depths.

He could never quite figure out why he seemed to always test a woman. Always issuing a challenge of some sort.

Rachel Mackenzie probably had a lot to do with his reactions, his wrestling persona being the very thing Rachel couldn't get enough of. His ex-wife could light a fire in the middle of a hurricane and keep it blazing with heat. That had been exactly what she had done to him, until he started being himself with her at home and in public. Rachel had wanted him to play the character he portrayed on an almost nightly basis. When he refused, the fire went out quicker than a blown-out match.

He prayed those same qualities Khristen exhibited on the flight would carry over into her writing of the article for *Plain Talk*. If she was the same Khristen Roberts, she would be spending more time with him on assignment. If not, he wasn't about to let her slip away from him. If he hadn't noticed the nametag on her carry-on, would he have wanted to pursue her further?

Of course. He'd be a fool not to.

That was yesterday afternoon. Now it happened to be a new day, a different situation altogether. Shadoe picked up a towel, wrapped it around his neck and sweat-drenched shoulder-length hair, and thought about the woman he hoped was his newest employee.

* * * *

Khristen dropped the bottle into the bag and smoothed the excess oil from her hands onto her face, gazing into the whale-shaped pool.

The beautiful eyes of the man from the plane seemed to appear as an apparition in the deep-blue-green pool water. Thoughts of him ran wild in her mind, and Khristen felt the warm wetness of desire grow deep between her thighs. She shivered from wanton desire. Something about him seemed familiar.

No. Surely, I would have remembered if we'd met before. His eyes, if nothing else, would have been burned into my memory.

It seemed as if she'd seen them, and the challenge in them, once before—a dare to defy him in any manner.

Challenges. That's what gave Khristen her drive. In her career, she had felt like a lamb lost in the fog in search of its home. She longed for the type of position that offered her the unexpected excitement of a contest each and every day.

Her current position at one of Madison's once top magazines came very close to fulfilling that yearning. It offered variety in its article context, and nine times out of ten, they didn't read like something out of *Miami Vice*. *Plain Talk* covered just about anything and sometimes everything. Still, something was missing.

She'd finally come to realize she wanted to be a staff member who did more than run around the office. She was going to spend the next few weeks thinking of a plan to convince Ric to move her up the ladder. One day, she would have her own byline.

Ric Scott, the magazine's editor-in-chief, had become the big brother she never had. He drank too much coffee in a day for one human being and stayed at the office until well past midnight. She worried about his excesses in both areas and feared one day she would walk into his office to find him slumped over his desk.

More than once, she had wondered why their relationship had never gotten past the big-brother stage. Deep in her heart, she knew it was the lack of emotional and sensual challenges. The spark she felt with a total stranger wasn't there with good ol' reliable Ric.

Khristen slid a pair of red-framed sunglasses

from the top of her head and perched them on her nose. She took a deep relaxing breath, leaned back, and forced the man's image out of her brain. She knew she had to let this challenge go for what very well could be the first time in her adult life. If letting go was at all possible.

For now, one thing she knew for sure. Absolutely no way was she going to become caught up in another romance. The last one had almost destroyed her, both emotionally and professionally.

* * * *

His shadow draped across her skin. He'd known he would find her; he'd never thought it would be connected to one of his businesses. He had thoroughly enjoyed seeing her sweat earlier, looking for a place to escape the dining room. If looks could kill, she should have laid him to rest before noon.

Now it was his turn, and he couldn't wait to see her reaction. It was going to get more interesting now that he'd decided in the length of time it took for him to reach her side that the game would start. He would have to proceed with caution before snaring her for himself.

Shadoe fought the temptation to pluck an ice cube from one of the glasses he carried and let it drip onto Khristen's sunburned flesh. A mischievous smile played on his lips as he visualized the response he would get. It would be fun, but they had already gotten off on a bad foot, and he didn't want to aggravate the situation further—or did he?

* * * *

"Khristen." Someone repeated her name, and as she stirred, raised his voice, calling to her again.

"Huh?" Sleepy eyed and well-burnt, Khristen was not sure what had drawn her out of a groggy sleep.

"What's your pleasure? Mai Tai, Piña Colada, or Aloe Vera?" Shadoe adjusted the two sweating glasses and one bottle on the tray he balanced with care.

Khristen shielded her eyes, suspiciously looking up at him. The touch of friendly sarcasm that had edged his over-exaggerated deep voice set off her warning light.

"Owweeee!" Pain and agony edged her voice, caused from the effects of too many hours in the sun and too little sunscreen.

"I've got just what you need."

"Like what?" Khristen grimaced, seeing the bottle of lotion and look of concern in his eyes.

Or is it lust?

"Aloe Vera. It's a great natural ointment with a cooling effect for skin that's on fire." He set the tray down on the small, round table next to her. "I could, ah, rub it in for you." Another teasing smile played on his lips as he picked up the bottle.

Khristen smiled back and looked into his eyes. How sexy and sure of himself he looked as he gazed over the rims of his sunglasses, daring her to resist his charm, challenging her.

"Actually, I have a better idea." She reached for the lotion and caught a look of satisfaction sweep over his face. With a crooked smile, she softly wrapped her fingers around the bottle and let them linger a moment too long before taking it into her possession.

"Mmmm, sounds very tempting." He moved in closer to her.

"It is," she said, reeling him in with her sweet, sexy tone, and placed her free hand on his bare chest, blocking his advance. As much as she'd love to feel his skin against hers, she wasn't about to play on his web.

"Fortunately, there's room for only one. You see, what I have in mind is, well..." She could see the anticipation grow in his eyes. "The ultimate total package of soothing the senses, everywhere, and all at once."

Gathering up her belongings, Khristen walked away, in pain. After only a few feet, she turned and gave him a look of triumph.

His deep, sexy laugh did nothing to dampen her victory.

CHAPTER 3

The smooth, oily bath water enveloped Khristen's sun burnt skin. She gathered her hair at the top of her head to keep it from the silky wetness now seeping just above her burning shoulders. The sting slowly left her tender skin while she caressed the slipperiness over her arms and legs with care.

She still couldn't believe that man had approached her with his little token of soothing liquid.

Who is he? How did he sneak up on me? Was I really sleeping that soundly? Why does he affect me the way he does?

It was all in those eyes the color of a clear, bright sea.

There was something about those deep, all-knowing eyes. She had the feeling she had seen those very eyes before. Something about this guy actually made her sweat in a delicious, haunting way. The worst part, in her mind, anyway, was that she wasn't afraid of him. His aggressiveness alone should have told her to run as far as she could in the opposite direction, but something kept her feet planted firmly on the ground.

A knock at the door startled Khristen and brought her out of her thoughts. She stepped from the lukewarm water well before she was ready to leave its warmth. Remnants of bubbles dripped on the floor as she wrapped a robe around herself and then hurried to answer the door.

"Who's there?"

"Room service, madam."

"Just a minute, please." Khristen checked to make sure the robe was securely tied, and then she released the lock and pulled open the door. "I didn't order."

A young man dressed in the proper hotel attire stood in the hallway holding a large vase full of tropical flowers. He walked past her, placed the delivery on the glass-topped table, and then flashed her a warm smile.

"But I didn't order these. You must have the wrong room."

"You are Khristen Roberts, aren't you?"

"Why, yes, but…"

"Then I have the right room. Enjoy your stay in Maui."

Bewildered, Kristen watched the door quietly close behind him. Her gaze took in the brilliant red-, yellow-, and violet-colored island flowers in the vase. She opened the single card and read aloud the three words scrolled on it. "We're tied. Shadoe."

Shadoe? Who in the world is Shadoe? She

thoughtfully tapped the card in the palm of her hand as she walked around the table. The only person who knew where she was staying didn't go by the name Shadoe. So that left only one deduction.

Despite herself, an amused smile seeped onto her face.

So that's his name. Well, at least he's persistent. How did he know who I was?

The plane...when my bag opened up, he must have seen my ID tag. So then, where did he get his information about my room number? The restaurant hostess from this morning? After all, he called me by my first name at the pool. No doubt he used his charm to finesse the information from the poor girl.

Then again, maybe he has a photographic memory of that darn baggage nametag. Or maybe he's just being sympathetic toward me for having fallen asleep poolside in the sun.

Remembering his lustful look earlier, she concluded that he was every bit a typical man.

This little fish is not taking the bait this time around.

* * * *

Shadoe had picked the most gorgeous flowers in the cooler. He didn't want to cause unnecessary suspicion in his own place of business, The Blue Seas Hotel, so he went to a nearby florist instead. This was his way of making sure she couldn't forget this afternoon, even if she tried. He wasn't sure whether she knew his name, but assumed with her brains, it would not be too hard for her to figure it out. He hoped she would be able to match his face with his signature.

Come to think of it, did she ever hear my name? Didn't the stewardess mention it?

Well, if she didn't catch it then, I'll make sure by the time she leaves for the mainland, my name will be etched in her mind and her soul for next to ever.

Damn, she looked so beautiful this afternoon, brilliant.

Women usually lusted after him. Not only for his body, which was in fantastic shape for a man in his position, but also because of his career.

Rachel had proved that. Every time he'd turned around, she had been on his heels like a puppy dog. It had gotten to the point where he couldn't even make an appointment for an interview without her tagging along. Why he ever let her convince him to marry her was beyond him now.

Yet...

He knew why. She was beautiful and a trophy to sport around, which was all he ever looked at for the short term. She definitely wasn't the kind of woman he would have pictured himself marrying if he decided it was time. In other words, his body had overruled reason where Rachel had been concerned.

She'd been very persuasive, both in and out of the bedroom, convincing him he needed her to keep things in his life in order. She'd kept his Johnson entertained at every possible moment.

Little had he known that she only cared about where he could put her on the social ladder. She didn't love him; only the size of his bank accounts had her heart. This had been one marriage too many for him after the hate-filled divorce that all but drained his bank account at the time.

Since then, he'd acquired silent partnerships through numerous connections in his chosen field. His work took him just about anywhere and at any given time. In fact, he traveled so much, being there at the hotel was the closest to a home base he had. Home always seemed to be a rented room.

At least this one belonged to him, in part.

As a matter of fact, he had been coming off a two-month road trip of nightly performances with the UWW and a tough new business deal of acquiring the small magazine in Madison, Wisconsin, when fate put him on that LA flight. If he hadn't missed the earlier connection in Madison, he wouldn't have met up with Khristen the other day.

Then, as luck would have it, he could hardly believe seeing her on the beach the next morning.

Will lady luck stay with me as she gets to know me better? Or will she simply turn away, thinking me nothing more than the arrogant fool? More important, will she respect me for who I am after she learns her future changed at my hands?

Why should I care?

* * * *

Khristen stepped out of the elevator and smack into a wall made of solid human flesh. Hard and masculine by the feel. His smell assaulting her senses reminded her of the ocean breeze...fresh and slightly salty, alluring to even the most celibate female.

"I'm-I'm really—" The words stalled somewhere between her vocal chords and lips.

Khristen's heart flip-flopped at the warmth radiating through his shirt and the firmness of his chest against her. Gazes met and smiles formed as she fiddled with her purse.

"Hey, that's okay. I do it all the time. Tell you what—if it will make you feel any better, I'll let you buy me a drink since you ran into me, okay?"

"Sorry, I can't. My mother always told me not to get into cars with strangers."

Now why in the hell did I just say that? Geez, made myself sound like a little girl set out on her first solo trip to the playground.

Her nerves crackled more with the growing moisture on her upper lip. What the heck was wrong with her, anyway? She acted like a giddy teenager, not a mature woman in her twenties.

She took a step back to break their physical connection, her nipples tingling with desire.

Stay cool. Don't lose it now. Not in front of him. He's just a man, not someone worth getting all hot and bothered about. Yeah, right. Then why in the hell am I? Answer me that!

"But I'm not really a stranger, after all. You do remember this afternoon, don't you? By the way, how is that back of yours?"

"Fine, thank you, even without your help." His nearness sent warm shivers through her, followed by an indistinguishable sweetness somewhere between lust, need, and want.

"Are you sure you don't want a drink or something? It's on me. I'd like to get to know a little something about the woman with whom I've been competing." His eyes twinkled with a mixture of desire and mischief. She felt as if she were held captive by their light.

"Competing? I was under the impression it was a mutual distrust of each other. My mistake." She turned to walk away but stopped when he stepped in front of her. She didn't dare look at his face. Instead, she gazed past his broad shoulder and out onto the veranda. She tried to think of her work and the reason for this trip.

"Would you agree to a truce, then, at least until we can see if it's worth continuing to dislike each other?"

The boyish grin on his face drew her to him. She felt totally helpless as she nodded her head in agreement.

He led her by the elbow to an empty table on the veranda where they could look upon the Pacific evening and watch the setting sun. It was something would-be lovers would do, not strangers who found it hard to be civil to one another.

Khristen tried to think of something—anything—to say as she watched him take his place opposite her. Never in her life had she seen a pair of jeans look as good as they did at that moment.

They sure don't make 'em look like that back home.

"I'm Shadoe Donovan. Are you here on business or pleasure?"

His deep, soft, sexy voice caught her off guard. "Huh?" She had been so absorbed in watching his muscles strain against his clothing she hadn't heard what he said. "Shadoe, the one who sent the flowers." It was more of a statement than a question.

He smiled at her, and she knew the answer even before he uttered the words. "One and the same. Are you here on vacation, or for professional reasons?"

"On vacation. My first to the islands." She diverted her gaze out to the ocean as the waitress approached them and then settled back into the chair.

Did he ask out of curiosity, or did he truly want to know?

It could be a trap she wanted to avoid—the hunter in pursuit of his prey. She wasn't about to fall victim to this hunt.

"What would you like to drink? White wine okay with you?"

"With ice, please." Khristen nodded in approval. She'd never really enjoyed wine at room temperature. She had to have it ice cold.

"We'll have a bottle of the house specialty wine and two chilled glasses." He leaned over the table as if the closer he got, the more he could see into her soul. "Vacation from where? No, let me guess. The Midwest, probably Illinois."

"Nope, try again."

"No. Wisconsin, then?"

"Yes, but you only had a few states before you'd have eventually gotten it right."

"Process of elimination. I've just returned from a business venture in that area. You don't look like a 'flatlander' to me. Besides, I asked at the front desk."

"Just what does a 'flatlander' look like?" She

raised her eyebrows at his left-handed remark. Judging from his indistinguishable accent, she didn't think he was from the Midwest.

Yet she knew just from the way he handled himself he must travel a lot. He was all business, with a touch of ease—no stiffness in dealing with people at all. Confidence oozed out of him like the center of a well-toasted marshmallow.

"Not like your standard corn-fed, milk-drinking farm girl." With a more serious note, he continued. "I want to apologize for my behavior on the plane the other day. As for this afternoon, well, I was just trying to be cute."

She shook her head. "Cute doesn't always work. The flowers softened the blow." A smile crossed her lips. "A little." No sense in letting him think he had won her over, which, of course, he had not.

"I'm glad you liked them."

The sunset's myriad of colors played breathtakingly on the water of the Pacific Ocean. The sky held a mixture of soft pastels while the sun reflected off the water, turning it a deep purple with a gold pink line seemingly running through the center. The colors calmed and mesmerized Khristen to distraction.

"It's beautiful, isn't it?" Khristen said in total awe of the natural loveliness. The scene provided the respite she needed for her raging hormones. Getting lost in the sunset might dampen the sexual urges building in her body.

"Yes, it is," replied Shadoe. "Just what is it that you do in Wisconsin, besides freeze in the winter?

What kind of work do you do?"

His expression told her he was genuinely interested. She wasn't sure, however, whether he had any other motives or not. In a split second, she decided his question was harmless enough.

"I work at a local magazine as a frustrated, glorified copy editor."

"Frustrated? How can being a copy editor be boring?" He picked up the half empty bottle of wine and refilled their glasses. "I would think some of the articles would be pretty interesting, if not informative."

Khristen took a sip of the wine. "I love the content of the work, but I want to be the one to research the stories, the one who draws the mental picture for the reader."

"What's the name of it—the magazine, that is—and what kind of things are in it?" He sat back, waiting for an answer from her.

She'd love nothing more than to taste the remnants of wine glistening on his lips. To lick the corners of his mouth and catch what sweetness was left behind. She looked away afraid he'd realize what she was on her mind.

"*Plain Talk.* It covers anything from women's issues to sports. Its objective is to bring to light as much about its topics as possible, pros and cons. We want our readers to see both sides, when possible, so they can decide for themselves on any particular issue."

* * * *

Bingo! She was his Khristen Roberts, after all. Now he'd have to be cautious and not let his building attraction for her push business out of the way. She would soon be a permanent business fixture in his life, and he didn't want to complicate that in any manner.

Business. Strictly business with this one.

"*Plain Talk*, you say?"

One of his many guardians must have heard his hopes. He could not be more pleased by her confirmation of working for the magazine. He was even a little worried now that he had a substantial connection to her. Would he be able to keep this purely professional?

I'll have to, that's all there is to it. He wasn't seeking any ties to her other than the magazine.

"That's right. Let's just say I'd rather be the painter of the pictures." She cocked her head to the side. "Are you all right?"

"Yeah. An artist at heart, eh?" He took a large gulp of the wine to settle his nerves. Lord help him if he got sidetracked on this deal, even if the idea of holding her in his arms for one night was a sweet one his body ached for.

"Of sorts."

Khristen finished the last of her wine and took a deep breath, making her breasts rise straight toward him.

Nice, firm and round, just begging to be touched and kissed... Back off, Donovan!

"Being a glorified typist is not my idea of how to spend the rest of my working days."

"Would you like more? I can order another." He reached for the near empty bottle.

"No, thanks. Two glasses is my limit. I wonder

what happened to our waitress."

"Why?"

"So I can pay for this." She fished around in her purse for some money.

Shadoe reached over the table and placed his hand on her busy one. "It's been taken care of."

"What?" She looked at him with surprise as the feel of her hand under his ignited his circuits. The palm of his hand covering the smallness of hers felt just right. Too right.

Khristen peered at him as he gave her his don't-question-me look. When she closed her purse, he withdrew his hand.

"I guess I'll take a walk along the beach before it gets too much later. It was nice meeting you, and thanks for the wine." Khristen pushed the chair out to leave.

Within a split second, Shadoe stood at her side with his hand upon the small of her back. She stepped away from him, and the show of shyness made him a little nervous.

Almost an excited sort of nervous. The kind you get when you are going to take your first roller coaster ride, when the idea takes your breath away with the anticipation of the ride, yet the fear of the speed with its dips and turns scares you just a little.

"I'll go with you."

"Thanks, but it's really not necessary. After all, I'm a big girl now, Mr… What did you say your name was?"

"Donovan. Shadoe Donovan. You shouldn't be walking alone at night."

Her gaze softened.

"Suit yourself," she said, though she didn't wait for him. She turned away and walked toward the veranda and beach joined by a patch of lush grasses.

Maybe it was time to step onto that roller coaster ride one more time. What harm could it cause him, anyway? Had he not hoped she would go for his offer? Of course he had, totally against his better judgment. Was he just being foolish about it, or overcautious?

No, more like stupid.

* * * *

Khristen slipped off her sandals before trading the grass for the soft white sand that sifted between her toes. The waves slapping along the shoreline sounded in perfect rhythm with the beating of native drums. The atmosphere of peace and tranquility dissolved some of the earlier tension she had felt from the man who now walked beside her.

"Tell me about yourself. After all, it's the only honorable thing to do after nosing into my world." Khristen's words stumbled into the silence that had enveloped them.

"Is it, now?" Shadoe teased, his words rolling like a rubber ball toward her.

"Yes, it is." A touch of authority rang through her words as they strolled through the sand.

Shadoe slipped his hand into hers, and she caught her breath. A smile came to her lips that she knew he could not see. Just the simple act of his hand wrapped around hers gave her a quiet satisfaction.

What if I pulled my hand away from his? Would the warmth and security still surround me? If I pull away, he'll have no recourse but to let me.

She would take whatever he did as a signal and cross that path when it happened.

"What would you like to know?" he asked.

"The usual. Anything and everything."

The warmth of his skin melted the coldness of her fear. Khristen didn't remove her hand from his. She actually tightened the grip slightly, enjoying the intimacy of the touch.

"Oh, I see. My life history," he said.

"But please, leave out the gory parts. Save those for another time."

His sudden silence spoke louder than any words could have. He wasn't going to volunteer any information; she would have to ask. He would probably handle each question as it came and reveal just enough to satisfy her, but no more than that.

"Are you on vacation, too? Although, now that I think about it, I doubt it. You seem to be pretty well known with the hotel employees."

She pulled her hand from the security of his and felt coolness where once there was warmth.

"I do a lot of traveling from the mainland to the islands."

"Business or pleasure?"

"Sometimes it's business but mainly for pleasure."

"What sort of business are you involved in? Monkey business?"

"Cute. No, I deal in, ah, public relations."

"How so?"

"All forms," he answered vaguely.

"Um-m-m. I guess that covers just about

RINGS OF PARADISE

anything," she said.

His evasive answers only ignited Khristen's curiosity, providing yet another challenge—one she had no intention of delving into. At least not at this given moment.

The night grew darker. The stars were like millions of flickering lanterns trying to break through the shadows. When they came upon some boulders, they sat down, watching a cruise ship slowly drift by. With all its many lights, it looked like a small floating city.

"You really surprise me." Khristen kicked at the sand, feeling the tiny granules slip between her toes. She missed the feel of his hand around hers; even though it had only been a minute or two, it felt like hours.

His hand had been strong and protective. His arms would be no different; she could tell. She wanted to feel what it was like to be in his arms, in the arms of a man who seemed to be interested in her, not what her monetary value was.

"I do, huh?" Mocked surprise echoed in his reply.

His voice echoed his enjoyment in this little game of cat-and-mouse. She knew he was more than a little amused, thinking she was fun to play with.

Well, maybe play is the wrong word in this case.

Khristen knew she couldn't get enough of this man.

She knew by the look on his face she'd revealed a little too much. She'd tried to hide it quickly, but not quickly enough. She wanted nothing more than to be in his arms and feel his lips against her own.

"Yes. You come off as so...so...now what's the word I'm looking for? Egotistical, full of yourself, like you're so great and could do no wrong." She was teasing him, and she enjoyed every second of it.

"I do?"

"Yes, you do. But then, you make a ninety-degree turn and act just the opposite. Why?"

"I'm a bit of a loner, I guess. That's not to say that I never socialize because I do. I'm usually with my business associates, though," he said.

"You seem to be so outgoing, once you decide to let go. I never would have guessed you to be that type." Khristen continued to nervously play with the grains of sand. "After all, you're on a beach in Hawaii with a woman you hardly know."

"I could say the same about you. Are you always this friendly with men you insult every time you see them?"

"We were talking about you, not me."

"Oh yes, I remember, my egotistical personality," he said. "It comes from not fully trusting a person I've just met. I can't afford to be used, so I don't let myself get into that situation."

"So, you act like a jerk instead of a person?"

"I'd like to think of it being more of a test of character."

"Whose character? Yours?" Khristen flung the words at him.

"No, the other person's. Especially if they're

female. In my chosen profession, I have to be careful of being recognized and then used. Sometimes, the public eye sees only what it wants to see. It doesn't care about you as a person but rather as a commodity. It's refreshing to meet someone who's just as spunky as I am and just as careful."

"Thus, the attraction to me? After all, in case you haven't noticed, I am a female."

"You don't have to remind me of what a female looks like." A smile twitched at one corner of his lips.

"And here I thought you only had one thing on your mind."

"Don't be too sure it's not on my mind." Shadoe's eyes filled with singed desire.

Khristen looked out to the quiet ocean, thinking of the complexity in this man she was fast growing to like. He had exposed some of himself to her—just enough to keep her interest, but not everything, by any means. The last thing she needed was to like him, even a little. She couldn't help it. That's what scared her most of all.

"It's late. I'd better be heading back," she said softly.

She took one last look at the dark ocean surf and headed back toward the hotel, with Shadoe no more than a half step behind her.

When they reached the hotel grounds, he slowed his pace then grasped her arm. They came face-to-face, soft breasts against hard muscle.

"Khristen, I..." His voice trailed off, and he held her with a gentle force.

"What is it, Shadoe?"

The warmth of him danced along the edge of her dress, sending shivers of desire through her. Her hair played along his shirt. Ever so slowly, gently, their lips met. Bodies locked in a heavenly embrace. The touch of his mouth coaxing hers to respond made her lightheaded. His hands cupped her face as his heated lips kissed each of her eyelids before trailing over her cheek and then down her neck straight to that little sensitive spot at her collarbone.

He huskily whispered her name through warm breath into her ear. His kisses, moist and hot, issued promises of satisfaction on the horizon if she cared to explore a little further.

Her earlobe became a morsel he could suckle and devour. Her skin burned with intense heated need; she felt she'd roast away into the soil and become cinders blended with the rich, dark dirt.

CHAPTER 4

Khristen drifted to the beat of a drum echoing in her ear. Her hand slid aimlessly over her temple and onto the pillow as the beat grew stronger and louder with each passing moment. She blinked her sleep-filled eyes and then realized the drum beating was actually someone knocking at the door.

Once again, her rest had been disturbed. Her clothes were wrinkled and pressed in all the wrong places from having slept in them all night. At the moment, she didn't give a darn what the person on the other side of the door thought of her appearance.

"Who is it?"

"Room service."

Not again.

She swung open the door and gazed at the man standing bright-eyed in front of her.

Once again, it was the bellboy from the other day. This time, he sauntered through, pushing a cart draped with a lacy white tablecloth. The tangy scent of pineapple juice and the aroma of bacon filled the room. A small bouquet of bird of paradise blooms sat in the middle of the cart, supporting a note card. The scent of the flowers mingling with the breakfast aromas filled her senses and made her stomach growl ever so slightly. She pressed her hand on the source, trying to muffle the sound.

"Are you sure?"

"Yes, madam."

"But..."

She stepped toward the cart for a closer look and shook her head in disbelief. No sense in trying to refuse; she knew she would lose the contest. This young man did his job well and with way too much enthusiasm so early in the morning.

"Have a good day." The bellboy smiled and left her standing in the middle of the room half-asleep.

She opened the small note card and read. *Morning. Meet me in the lobby at twelve-thirty. Shadoe.*

The card, held securely between her fingers, found its way to her lips. The memory of Shadoe's kiss warmly rushed through her, and a smile crossed her face. The kiss had been soft and gentle before smoldering desire burned her tender lips as their bodies fit perfectly together, melting into one. Other than that, they were anything but a perfect match.

They were two different types of people. He was worldly and sophisticated in his manner, where she was simple and liked things homey and comfortable. He barged ahead, while she weighed the situation before making a move.

Even so, it had been all she could do to keep

him from getting any closer last night.

That kiss absolutely was the kiss of all kisses. She imagined what making love to this man would be like. She could and would imagine it each time he came to mind, each time his eyes ignited desire in her. No one would come remotely close to the level of passion he singed into her—a passion that would have to be placed back on the shelf when she returned home in a few days. The memory would join the extinguished fire left three years ago by Dane.

* * * *

Shadoe watched as Khristen walked through the breezeway.

Damn, she is a beautiful woman.

She kept her spirit on a tight rein, but he could tell it wanted release. Strip away her fears, the apprehension in her eyes, and she would soar. But something, he wasn't sure what, wouldn't allow her the opportunity to do so. He hoped his plans would change all that.

Last night had been the worst—and best—night he could remember. His controlled resistance had been tested well beyond his limits when it came to this woman he found so damn sexy. The long, cold shower he'd taken had done little to suppress the lust in his heart.

The kiss may have been forward, but he couldn't stop his body, once things got started. He couldn't resist taking Khristen in his arms. At that particular time, he'd been going down for the count. A loud *"one…two…three!"* had resounded through his soul as he'd felt the control leave him.

He wanted to taste her soft wine-tinged lips for just a moment—just long enough to satisfy his thirst. He'd never counted on taking it any deeper than a friendly gesture.

She'd been so responsive, warm, and sweet to taste. Her lips made him forget he was her boss, made him forget about business. She filled him with a wild desire to lay her down on the beach and finish what had been started.

If someone hadn't happened along at that precise moment, it would have been too late for thinking. Their indentations would have been left on the sand before the tide washed them out to sea in the morning.

That wasn't the only thing that would have been washed away. Any hope of a business relationship with Khristen would have gone with it. He thanked his lucky stars for the interruption and his loss for words on the walk back to the hotel.

Today, he would have a chance to put things in proper order, business before pleasure. Ric Scott's call would come within minutes of their lunch. Regardless of what Scott warned him about, he wanted to make this little business venture work.

The more time they spent together for non-business reasons, the more he forgot about business, and forgetting about business was something he wasn't about it give up, whether it be the ring or his personal business. The longer they stayed on the islands, the more they had to lose.

* * * *

Khristen spotted him in less than a second; she only had to follow the origin of the "being stared at" feeling touching her the moment she walked through the door.

Shadoe sat at a table on the veranda near a section of the garden. His hair hung freely in the light breeze, and he smiled when he caught sight of her. Shivers racing through her, she smiled back and then took the most direct route to his table.

"Hi," Shadoe whispered as he stood while she seated herself.

"Hello. Thanks for breakfast and the beautiful flowers. Out of all exotic ones, those are my favorites. They always look so mystical to me, as if they're ready to take flight."

"Good. I'm glad you liked them, and I thought you might need something to eat after the wine last night. May I order for you?" Shadoe picked up the menu and glanced at it. "I never will look at those particular flowers again without waiting for wings to flutter open."

Shadoe ordered her a plate of fresh pineapple, kiwi, melon, honeydew, and cottage cheese. The plate of chilled fruit was just what she needed to cool down her body temperature. If the warmness of her cheeks were any indication, she knew the rest of her skin must be glowing the same pinkness.

"About last night, I'm..." He hesitated when a waiter set a telephone down in front of Khristen, indicating there was a call for her.

"Me?" When the waiter nodded, she picked up the receiver, wondering whether everything was in order back home.

"Hello... Ric, slow down. You're talking so fast I can't understand a word you're saying... Yes, that's better... Sold?" The word was barely comprehensible to her.

Her body shook from the news, and a hundred things ran through her mind. Would there be a job waiting for her once she got back home? If not, what would she do? Unemployment was up and jobs scarce. The thought of flipping burgers after working for the magazine didn't sound appealing at all.

"To whom? When? Just the other morning?" She swallowed the large lump lodged in her throat. "Okay, okay...What changes? You're kidding."

She laid the receiver back in place, shaking. She pinched herself in the thigh to make sure she wasn't dreaming, that she hadn't imagined the news Ric had just given her, news about the magazine that she never would have believed.

Well, at least she'd gotten answers to her unspoken questions. She'd never dreamed she would be promoted.

"Khristen?" Shadoe reached over to touch her hand where it still lay on the instrument, his voice coaxing her out of her thoughts.

"I'm sorry, Shadoe. I didn't mean to..." Tears filled her eyes. The pools under the lids threatened to spill over her lashes. If she blinked, they would leave a track down her cheeks, and her nose would be as red as Rudolph's.

"What's wrong? What has upset you so?" he asked.

"The magazine. It seems someone walked in off the street and bought it. We didn't even know it was for sale. Adding to the oddity of it all, my position is the only one that's changed. Other than the ownership, that is." She felt like she'd just taken a ride on a roller coaster. Her life raced full steam ahead, and she didn't have the power to slow it down for a moment to think.

Her job as copy editor was no more, the money she had spent on this vacation to decide how to convince Ric she was capable of more—wasted. Well, maybe not totally wasted. She had met Shadoe, after all.

"Don't tell me you've been fired. Khristen, I'm so sorry. If there's anything..."

"No, as a matter of fact, just the opposite. I've been somewhat promoted," she said through a nervous chuckle.

"Hey, that's great! To what?"

"Reporter." Confused excitement echoed in the single word as reality started to set in. Some unknown person had given her the chance to work as the word painter she'd dreamed of being since starting with the magazine. She would be the one to give their readers a visual—the one to create the story and present the facts.

Reporter! I'm now a reporter!

Laughter spilled from her, and she held back tears. Perfect—her life was now perfect.

"Are you serious? See, if you wait, things fall into place. Patience, good work, drive, determination, all of that. Wow, and to think I've just experienced a dream come true for someone. What a rush!" He handed her a napkin to dry her face.

"Yeah, I guess dreams do come true, after all,"

she remarked. She dabbed at the tears and her nose, thanking the guardian angel who'd heard and granted her this wish—wish to be something more in her life, to make things better for her than it had been growing up in a blue-collar family struggling to make it from paycheck to paycheck.

Staring at a busy hummingbird, she began to think about the phone conversation. It dawned on her what else Ric had said. She knew absolutely nothing about the topic. Or even where to begin. Were there even any reference materials available? Most likely not, unless they were written by someone whose name included something like "Smasher" in it.

"What's your first assignment going to be? Some female-type thing, I bet, like the latest French fashion or redecorating on a budget."

"You won't believe this one." She paused then looked him in the eye and held her breath a second before the words spilled out in a rush. "Pro wrestling!"

"What?"

"Can you imagine? Professional wrestling. I haven't even seen this stuff on TV, now I've got to attend live matches and report on the pros and cons of the sport." She played with the plate of fruit.

"Such as?"

"The usual controversy. Is it fake? Are the matches fixed? Is it real blood or not? Do they cut themselves? Ric said it's a fast way to get those people upset with you, to put it mildly."

"Well, you'll have to express your indifference and write what you see, not what you don't see."

"I know. That'll mean attending matches all over the country. Several of them. In fact, Ric said I have to be back in Wisconsin by the end of the week." Remorse edged her tone but didn't do a thing to stop her hands from shaking. Her vacation would be reduced to days rather than weeks, and she was just getting to know a little more about Shadoe. They were quickly becoming comfortable with the possibility of a friendship.

She found she liked Shadoe despite all her misgivings about him. Underneath his exterior lived a likeable man who made her want to stay on the island forever.

This man who had been a pain in the butt had turned out to be just the opposite. He was considerate and not the arrogant fool she'd first thought he was. She actually found him to be the type of man she could envision herself getting serious about somewhere down the line. Now all of that might come to an end and all for a dream come true.

"Oh, man, just when I felt my charm getting through that wall of yours, too! Are you sure he said the end of the week, meaning tomorrow night?"

"Yeah."

"You said that this could be the first installment?"

"From what he said, my ultimate goal is to get an interview with some guy who's ranked in the top ten in some federation. I'm to get that interview at all costs—do anything, absolutely anything to get him to open up and talk about the business."

Khristen went on to explain what she knew,

which included nothing about the sport. When Shadoe reassured her she would do just fine, her spirits lifted. He even went so far as to suggest that she get an interview with a few of the other athletes before tackling her main target. It might help her get the feel of how they acted and how to handle them.

As he continued to give her advice, she numbed with amazement at how their friendship had bloomed in such a short time. No matter how strongly she tried to avoid being around him, it seemed they were destined to be matched as friends. She would love nothing more than for their friendship to continue after they parted ways.

"I wish there was something I could do to help, but being a journalist is one field I know almost nothing about," he said. A sexy smile played on his mouth. "But there is one activity I know a little bit about I want to share with you before you have to leave...snorkeling."

* * * *

Khristen's heart hammered with excitement as Shadoe sped along the highway in the rented Jeep Cherokee. In the mid-afternoon, the traffic flowed with ease along the shoreline. Both she and Shadoe were dressed for a day at the beach—Khristen in her red-and-white one-piece, which she partially covered with a white calf-length gauze skirt, and Shadoe in a pair of yellow-and-black shorts with a matching short-sleeved shirt.

The radiance of the sun nearly blinded her while the warm North Pacific salt breezes brushed against her face. Khristen's hair blew free and wild, as if it would become entwined with his at any moment.

"Are you always so color-coordinated?" she teased, surveying the pair of canary-yellow-and-black sunglasses perched on his nose. "You look like a big yellow jacket."

"That's so people know they'll be stung by a powerful bee if they cross me." A boyish shyness crossed the smile on his face as he pulled the jeep through some foliage and onto a small, private, sandy beach.

If she didn't know where to look, she never would've found it from the road. They were absolutely the only people there.

"This is my personal escape from the tourists. It's difficult to really enjoy the island's beauty when there's a lot of pushing and shoving going on all around you."

Khristen looked into his eyes. He had a way of making her feel safe, but she didn't know quite how to react to him. Her body blazed with desire, but she knew she should keep her head about her. She'd be gone tomorrow morning, and odds were they'd never see one another again.

Shadoe jumped from the jeep and unloaded the needed gear from the back.

"Come on, before it gets too late."

He's nice. Too bad. You know what happened the last time with Dane.

She watched Shadoe jog away from the jeep.

He raced toward the sandy beach and waved at her before Khristen could even unbuckle her seat belt. By the time she caught up with him, he had stripped away the shorts and revealed a pair of swimming trunks. A water mask tilted on his head while the mouthpiece perched in front of the eye gear. It took all she could do not to laugh aloud.

"What's so humorous?" Shadoe stood with hands on hips, his eyes narrowed.

"You are!" she laughed. She had to dodge the pair of fins he tossed her way, or they would've hit her square in the chest.

"You look pretty cute dressed up like that. Sort of a fish out of water," she said.

"Oh yeah! Well, by the time you get ready, we'll look like a couple of mismatched bookends, won't we?"

Khristen pulled off her skirt and slipped into her equipment. Her process slowed to a snail-like pace while her attention focused on Shadoe putting their clothing neatly in an athletic bag.

How can a guy look sexy just packing clothing?

"Well, look at you. Now you look like a 'fishette' out of water."

He closed his eyes just before the sand Khristen playfully kicked hit him squarely in the face.

"Why, you...! You're going to pay for that!" Shadoe dropped the mask onto the sand and chased Khristen into the water. Once in the clear blue water, her pace halted when his arms wrapped around her, and the force of his body knocked her face down in the ocean.

They emerged in one another's arms, laughing like teenagers, smiling as their noses touched. Desire filled Shadoe's eyes before their wet, salty lips met, and fiery need surrounded them in a sea of deep blue water.

Shadoe scooped her into his arms and carried her through the water to lie on the sandy white beach. He gently lifted the mask and snorkel from her wet head, gazed into her eyes, then kissed the droplets of moisture from her lashes.

She trembled, not from the cold, but from the sweet anticipation of what could be hers for at least one night. She propped herself on her elbows. "Shadoe—"

"Sh-sh-sh." He lightly touched her lips with a single finger and traced their edges in a slow deliberate manner. She trembled and shivered as feelings long put away soared through her body.

He coaxed her mouth with his, encouraging her to allow the passion to respond again. Every move was as one. Khristen submerged deeper into a sea of tranquility until, alas, he pulled her from the depths, back to the surface, away from the sweet drowning she hadn't thought to fight.

Still trembling from the kiss, Khristen forced herself to sit up, though her senses quaked from his touch. She wrapped her arms around her knees and laid her head on them to watch Shadoe's face. For a brief instant, it seemed that all the self-confidence always present had disappeared, leaving him vulnerable.

"Shadoe, I'm, well, not..." she began.

She stumbled to find the right thing to say, feeling unwarranted blame and embarrassment surface for losing control of a situation, thankful that Shadoe had the foresight to stop before they'd gone too far.

What had she done wrong? Had she allowed

him too much freedom? It was just a kiss, after all, no different than the night on the beach. She wanted him to touch her, to feel him claim her as his own. To put out the wildfire burning through her loins, threatening to incinerate her fences.

"It's just...it's been a long time since…" she continued.

Painful memories of Dane caused tears to stream down her cheek as she searched through the words caught in the back of her throat.

"Khristen, stop. Please stop crying. I didn't mean any disrespect." His own self-blame came through his words. "I was going with the flow."

Khristen drew never-ending circles in the sand and then looked out into the openness of the late afternoon sun shimmering off the darkening water. She felt as if she was on a Ferris wheel that spun faster and faster.

Everything was going too quickly. She really liked him, but enough for intimacy? A one-night—day—stand? Her heart and body told her *yes,* while her mind now fought back with repeated *nos.*

"Shadoe, when I give myself fully to a man, it'll be because I wanted to. There must be some sort of an emotional tie involved. I don't want to get caught up in the moment. That's why it's called 'making love,' isn't it?"

Shadoe raised an eyebrow and kissed her turned-up nose. "I can appreciate how you feel, but there's more than one way to give yourself fully. There's more to any relationship than just sex," he assured her.

"I realize that, but we've only known each

other for a few days. I do like you. You've become a friend; I don't want a moment of sexual desire to ruin it."

Another tear slipped down her cheek before he could kiss it away.

"Khristen, you've no idea what you've said means to me. Maybe someday, you'll come to understand me better and the reason for my actions with you these past few days."

"You sound as if we'll see each other again."

"We will, I guarantee it."

"I hope so, Shadoe."

* * * *

Khristen woke with a start, her breathing shallow and fast, the flimsy nightie clammy against her trembling, moist flesh. She licked her dry lips and begged her heart to be still. Her thoughts flashed back to Shadoe, the beach. She'd never felt happier or more scared in her life. These past few days with him had relaxed her. She'd even stopped bantering with him, a sign of trust not easily given by either of them.

Now, in just a few hours, she'd be on her way back to that other world—a world of confusion and constant competition, a world without him. Reluctantly, she got out of bed to get ready to leave this small piece of Hawaiian paradise.

At the hotel's front door, Shadoe caught Khristen's eye as she stepped off the elevator. She couldn't decide whether to be happy or sad to see him.

He stepped toward her. "Need a lift?"

"That's not really necessary. Besides, I

wouldn't want you to go out of your way."

"Now, what else have I got to do besides escort a pretty little lady to the airport?"

"A heavy date, maybe?"

"Yeah, at least a couple of tons or more."

* * * *

They drove in silence to the airport and kissed goodbye as the last boarding call echoed through the waiting area. Shadoe had bypassed security and gained access to walk her to her boarding gate. Khristen turned and waved just before passing through the entrance. Shadoe blew her one last kiss.

In silence, he watched the plane taxi onto the runway. A surge of wickedness seeped into his body as he chuckled aloud.

Khristen sure did have a way of making him lose control of his desire to touch her.

He recognized the pain in her eyes whenever the flame flickered. She tried to keep it buried deep inside, and he tried to coax it out in the open. The best way to rid your mind of something painful is to face it head on, which was exactly what he wanted to help her do.

He wanted to feel her body next to his each time they were together, but there was always something to stop it from happening. Maybe he was finally putting business before pleasure. Maybe this venture would work, after all. Maybe, just maybe, he could keep his heart intact through the entire thing.

He had to call Scott and start the wheel of truth in motion. He had to set the record straight before time ran out.

He watched the plane, now a small speck, disappear into the sky, and then made his way to a vacant pay phone, pulled his cell phone from its belt clip, and punched in the number.

"Your phone call happened to come while I was there with her. I wish you had told me she'd gone to Maui. Or even what she looked like; I could have handled it differently... Anyway, it's a job well done... No, she doesn't suspect. Why should she? Yes, I know it's not a game, and it could blow up in my face." Shadoe listened for a few more minutes, staring off into space. "I'll be there in a few weeks, and I want you to keep this between us for now. I'll keep in touch with more instructions... I do know I want her in Cedar Rapids and then some time with the federation. Yes, I know you care about her feelings, but who's the boss here?"

Shadoe disconnected the call, mumbling, "The test of character now begins."

CHAPTER 5

Khristen hunched over the computer, keying in her article, strong, determined clicks erratically echoing in the dimly lit corner of the hotel room.

They've been called actors...entertainers in their own sport. Their audience loves and hates them. Young and old alike join to cheer and jeer their favorites.

Professional wrestlers...true athletes? Just entertainers? Or a mixture of both?

When I walked into this Wisconsin arena on a clear summer night, I found the crowd anticipation as thick as a dense fog rolling in from London. The concession area hummed with fans feverishly buying posters, scarves, T-shirts, mugs, and souvenir programs, while women and young ladies drooled over the posters of half-naked males.

Members of the crowd voiced differences of opinion until the faintly heard opening bell. On command, loyal fans emptied the concession area to take their assigned seats. I took mine in the second row from the ring.

In spite of my gallant attempts to curb my excitement, my pulse accelerated at the announcement of the first battle. The two contestants made their way into the ring, the fever of the crowd caught, and cheers roared.

In the first five or six minutes, it became clear, even to this untrained eye, this match would be anything but exciting. A youthful Adonis-type figure climbed into the ring, quickly overtaken by the veteran twice his size sent out to give the young rookie a lesson in the fine art of "entertaining."

Cheers and jeers mingled with chants of "booorrring" as the opponents eyed each other. It wouldn't take much time to see just how long, or should I say short, the young warrior would be in the business.

"Damn," Khristen uttered at the ring of the phone and stopped pounding away at her keyboard. Her thought processes totally out the window, she sighed deeply to control her irritation. "It's gonna take me at least ten minutes to get back into my thoughts after only a second of pulling me out. What else is going to prevent me from finishing this assignment?"

I should have unplugged the phone.

"Hello." Her voice held that edge of irritation building inside.

"Hi, Khristen." The male voice came softly and filled with longing over the telephone line.

"Shadoe? Is that you? How did you know where I was staying?" She couldn't help being surprised by how easily her mood changed. "What a nice surprise. Unexpected, but nice."

She played with the phone cord and pictured the boyish cockiness of his grin while she waited for an explanation that only he could come up with. She missed seeing him and hearing the laughter, which followed him around. Who would've thought he'd ever call her? She certainly never expected to hear the sound of his voice again after leaving Hawaii.

"Give me more credit than that, would ya? It's not so hard to call every hotel and motel in Madison, is it?" He sounded hurt that she would ask such a question. "And besides, what are you doing in a hotel? I thought you had an apartment there."

"I didn't want to be bothered with phone calls. Evidently, it didn't work, did it?" she asked, her stomach flipping over with suspicion.

Oh God, do I have a stalker on my hands now? I've read about this sort of thing happening to women. What if I'm not his first victim, and he was out to get me.

No, I told Ric about him; he told me not to be alarmed.

So, why am I? I trust Ric's judgment; he's never led me astray before. And he's so good-looking and sexy and sweet and...

"Remember, I'm a man of many resources." Shadoe paused "Actually, I called the magazine and convinced some guy there I needed to find you. He told me where you were. How was it? The matches, I mean."

Her heart beat faster at the realization of his

words.

He remembered the magazine's name and actually went looking for me.

The very thought brought warmth into her heart, igniting the need in her core. Maybe there was hope, after all, and Cupid had indeed looked her way.

"Okay, I guess. I just find it hard to believe these guys let themselves be abused like that. I saw some falsity out there tonight."

Oops, thinking out loud again. Have to learn to keep those thoughts to myself.

She lay across the bed on her stomach, legs bent up at the knee, kicking her feet. She felt like a teenager from an old beach party movie.

"Are you going to write that?"

"Of course. What kind of a journalist do you think I am? I have to say what I saw. But, I can't base it all on one night at the 'fights,' now, can I?" She rolled over onto her back, feeling all of sixteen. If only she had a girlfriend to call and giggle with, the feeling would be complete.

"Now I suppose you'll be some sort of a 'groupie' for these guys. You'll be following them around like a puppy dog and hanging out in the back just waiting for a glimpse of who knows what. A real wrestling fan through and through. Fan first, journalist second."

"What the heck? Are you kidding? No way! These guys have enough women hanging on them without someone like me. I'm here to do a job, and that's it. Until I can get a deep, inside look, I'll keep playing the role I've been assigned—spectator and writer. Nothing more. Nothing less."

She had no intention of becoming a notch on someone's boot, no matter how attractive he may be. The idea hadn't even occurred to her.

* * * *

Shadoe felt relief as her words sunk deep into his beating heart. He'd really hoped she'd be as honest as possible with the article, and that he wouldn't have to worry about losing her. He liked the guys he worked with, for the most part. It was just that some of them liked to exercise their other talents outside the ring. Others wanted to add more notches to their wrestling boots through their charming ways.

"Have you caught up with...what's his name?" he asked.

"Flame."

He couldn't miss the annoyance in her tone. As if he'd caused her the inconvenience of not waiting for her return before starting the match. He told himself her irritation was due to her feelings about the assignment, nothing more.

"Yeah, that's it. Was he on the list of performers?" Shadoe smiled to himself, knowing full well his own role in all of this.

"Card. You mean card, and yes, he was. I missed seeing his match. My throat was parched, and the lines were long and slow. Before I got back, Flame was in and out of the ring."

"So you missed his whole bout?"

She hasn't even seen me in action yet. So she has no clue we're one and the same. This should be interesting to hear.

"Yes, but I did notice the fans are kind of wishy-washy towards him. That much I could hear. It seems there's a love-hate feeling for the guy. It'll be interesting to see him in action and find out what all the noise is about."

"You haven't formed the love-hate feeling, huh? Given time, you most likely will, same as everyone else has."

"I'm not sure what you're driving at, Shadoe. Care to explain it to me," she asked, clearly annoyed by his flippant assumption.

He'd opened his mouth and spoken without thinking—a bad habit he'd picked up since going back to Hawaii. Ever since they'd met, he'd been unnerved and more than a little out-of-sorts in his universe. She made him believe in things he'd thought he never would again.

Family. Children. Retirement.

A moment of silence floated through the phone lines. "I'm passing through town, and thought maybe... Have you had anything to eat yet?" He tried to calm the rapid beating of his heart at the thought of spending a few hours with her. It'd been weeks since he'd seen her off at the Maui airport. Up until now, he hadn't realized how much he'd missed her. His heart was sending subtle reminders to the tip of his penis.

"I've really got to get this done, Shadoe, while it's fresh in my mind," she said.

"So, you're turning me down, then?" Laughter edged his question as he attempted to conceal the disappointment.

"How about a rain check?"

"But, it's not raining," he protested.

"I thought I heard thunder pounding in the sky just a few moments ago," she countered.

"You must be mistaken. The stars are bright, and the moon is full. Not a cloud in the sky."

Yeah, thunder that sounded a little like jealousy to me. Slightly unrealistic, don't you think, old man.

"No storm clouds at all?"

"Come on, Khristen. You have to eat. Super reporter you're not...yet," he teased.

"Okay, you win. I guess I could use a small break. Just the mention of food brought a rumble to the pit of my stomach."

"Great! Give me five minutes."

* * * *

The click of the phone echoed in Khristen's ear before she could respond. She hesitated a moment and was about to return to her laptop when someone knocked on the door.

"Great, more interruptions."

She marched over to the door, prepared to drive home the point that she hadn't requested anything. Instead, she opened the door to find Shadoe standing in well-fitting cowboy-cut blue jeans, white T-shirt, and a pair of well-worn ropers. All combat readiness evaporated along with her frustration at continuously being interrupted.

"Shadoe, you said five minutes, not five seconds!"

"I can always leave and come back."

"Why bother? You've made it this far. Come on in."

Shadoe pushed a meal cart into the room and

between the two double beds.

"Get over here and eat before it gets cold."

"You took a chance that I'd agree to see you, as usual." Khristen reached out to uncover the platter in front of her. "So what have we got here anyway? Ouch!"

"Now, now...you mustn't touch," he said. He winked and then removed his hand from the top of hers.

"Oh, the look-but-don't-touch routine. How typical," she teased back. "Trying out a new approach?"

"Mmm, maybe. Everything else from the past has failed, so I thought food might pave the way. Besides, this way I get to do the honors in providing you with a meal fit for a queen and her king."

"Right...king and queen of what, exactly? The 'Peanut Gallery'?"

"You'll see… Ta da!" He snapped off the server cover to reveal two hamburger containers and two large fries from the local fast food joint. "Mmmm, grease. What a deliciously prepared meal for royalty such as we." He exaggerated. Khristen held her stomach; her laughing cramped the muscles.

"Oh, your Royal Highness, how well you provide for your lady." Khristen knelt on one knee, took his hands in hers and kissed the tops of them like any royal subject in a movie would.

"Enough, enough. Let's eat." Shadoe popped open a burger container.

"How'd you know I'd be in town? For all you knew, I could've been on assignment in

RINGS OF PARADISE

Minnesota...or Canada, for that matter."

Khristen watched for any facial expressions that might give him away, but as usual with Shadoe, none did. Just when her lust-heated blood came down from a rapid boil, he showed up to turn the flame back to high. It had been a long four weeks without him around.

Fun and games are over. I want some answers, and I want them now.

The real question was whether the answers would be straight, or mysterious like the man himself?

Will I catch him in a lie? How true did his answer ring a few minutes ago? Miss Untrusting, that's what I'm acting like.

Nah, just honing my reporter skills, nothing more.

"Like I said, I arrived here for business, so I called the magazine. Let's go and do something," he said.

"Shadoe, I have a deadline to meet. I really can't. I've got to get back to work. Thanks, anyway."

"Khristen, you need to have fun. Please, for me." His gaze turned soft and pleading. It was the same look she'd found hard to resist only a few short weeks ago when their friendship took root—roots that continuously grew stronger even in his absence from her tiny world.

His large hands rested with ease on her shoulders. His long, strong fingers massaged her knotted muscles, melting the past few hours away. The built-up tension seemed to work its way down her body to another area where lust could not so easily be persuaded to go away. She pulsed with each contraction of his hand on her knotted muscles. The trail of kisses he left on her neck and shoulder weakened her resistance.

"It just doesn't do any good to say no, does it? You're worse than a spoiled little boy." She melted into his arms and kissed him.

"That I am... Spoiled rotten to the core but every inch a man," he whispered, returning her kiss with the flick of his tongue against hers. The electrical current the simple, sensual act created sent her over the edge. She clung to him for dear life.

"You really make it hard, you know. But, I can't. Not tonight, Shadoe. I've got this article to finish before I can even think about having fun of any kind. Please understand. It's my work." She purred from his touch when the last of his warmth lingered, fueling her longing for more than a shoulder rub.

"A career woman—just what I need in my life. Another time then, my fair lady. Another time." He kissed her cheek and left with a smile on his face.

The door closed softly, and Khristen sat at her computer attempting to read over what she had accomplished before the uninvited, but welcome, interruption.

She pushed her feelings aside and got back to the business at hand—her first article.

A face rubbed along the ropes, showing hardly a red mark from my viewpoint as over-exaggerated arms went into the air and falsely expressed pain flashed on the young man's face. At this point so early in the card, the crowd became more entertaining than the bout itself.

Outcome? The veteran walked away the victor. How could it be any other way? The rookie had been demolished out there. Nothing seemed to work. Control was never his from the start. Result: Another lesson learned.

"Not unlike Shadoe and myself." She looked at the cart and the empty food containers he'd left behind along with his warmth. "He definitely takes control; before I know it, I'm following him down the yellow brick road to Oz."

Match number two began. While the night's ring announcer entered the squared circle—don't ask me why they call a squared roped area a circle—and signaled for the bell, I thought of the job I was sent to do. The names of the next two gladiators came over the microphone.

The boos and sneers echoing through the hall, The Terror made his way into the ring, his temper glowing. This two-hundred-seventy-pound former street gang member from the kitchens of hell yelled, pointing at a couple of guys who acted ready to take him on. Experienced or not, they were ready to show their manhood. Involved with those guys, The Terror didn't notice the catcalls had quickly changed to cheers until it was too late.

A man outfitted in a shocking-pink-and-black spandex getup jumped into the ring while his opponent wasn't watching. His partner had taken quite a beating at the hands of this adversary the night before. Revenge was now his for the taking.

The task proved not to be an easy one, for the

two ancient warriors were evenly matched in size and strength. Body slams were countered. Missed flying elbows landed on the mat or a turnbuckle. Body sweat sprayed out onto people sitting ringside. The match was action-packed; each of the competitors like stallions out to prove who was the fittest of the herd.

"Stallion. Shadoe. Definitely a close comparison in sleekness and maleness... Cool it, Khristen! Get to work and quit doing this," she scolded, forcing her attentions back to wrestling in the ring and not elsewhere.

As the twenty-minute time limit drew to an end, The Terror pinned one-half of the Love Channel for a three count. With his shoulders flat on the battlefield, the fallen warrior could hardly believe the "war" had ended. Or had it?

"Love Channel? I know who'd I like to have conquering my love channel, and I let him walk out the door a few minutes ago. Damn, what was I thinking, turning down some time with him after all these weeks?

"Okay, so I'm an adult totally devoted to writing this damn exposé!"

Sounds of disappointment echoed in the air, overshadowed by deep, evil-sounding music signaling the appearance of the tag team called Darken Death. These two guys looked like a couple of misplaced gladiators from ancient times. Dressed in black leather and studded hooded masks, they reflected something from ancient Rome, if not before.

Cheers quickly boomed as a lone wrestler

entered the front lines and began to speak, telling us all that his partner wouldn't be there due to an injury at the hands of Darken Death, and another tag team would fill in for them. Two painted warriors just as huge as the champions defending their kingdom stepped out from the darkness through a new wave of killer music.

The Painkillers hit the ring. Delivering forearm after forearm until the newest members of the UWW cleared the ring of their opponents. My pulse raced, and my heart beat a little faster and harder. We all watched with nervous anticipation as we waited for the team of Darken Death to make the next move.

* * * *

Khristen woke with the sun in her eyes. Her face rested against her folded arms, which were supported on the small, round hotel table. Her head pounded with a dull ache, and the annoyance of the ringing phone hurt her ears. She felt like she had been drinking the night away instead of working to near-exhaustion the night before.

"Hello." The pain reflected through her sleepy voice.

"Khristen?"

"Who is this?" She pulled the curtains shut to keep the morning sun from continuing to blaze into the room. "Have you any idea what time it is? Just because the sun's up doesn't mean I am."

"It's Ric. What's with you?" asked the editor-in-chief.

"Too much work. Why?"

"It sounds like too much party to me."

"Wrong. Just because you're my boss doesn't

mean you can call at the crack of dawn." Khristen stifled a yawn and then stretched her sleepy muscles. "Ric, what's up, anyway?"

"How's the article? Finished?" he asked. "And, for the record, I'm your friend first, boss second."

He sounded concerned.

Probably worried I won't be able to meet today's deadline.

She glanced down at the black-and-white screen and then scrolled through the previous night's work. She'd get the article written and to the office in time. He had nothing to worry about—a fact she knew, but he didn't.

"It's close."

Shadoe's surprise dinner had not only put her behind but also caused her mind to wander on more than one occasion. He had this incredible way of taking over any situation or opposition with ease. If he wasn't already in politics of some sort, he should be. He could be very persuasive when he wanted to be—sweetly persuasive.

"Deadline's today at four-thirty... Will it be ready?"

"It'll be there by close today. Is that why you called? To check up on the article?"

She flopped face-first on the bed. Didn't he have any faith in her ability to complete the assignment? She'd get the article done in more than enough time, even if work was the last thing she had on her mind. At the moment, all she wanted was the long, hot bubble bath and soothing music for the pain in her head that would have to wait for couple more hours.

"Good. And if you'd been actually listening to me instead of fuming because I woke you up, you wouldn't be asking me that question. I just want you to know things have changed."

Okay, now he's going to get to the real reason why he called while the sun was still the color of an orange.

"How's that?"

"You're going on tour."

"Right… With whom? Did David Lee Roth schedule a comeback tour?"

"You wish. No, not exactly. But just as exciting, I bet." His voice sounded unsure, even though he tried to hide it, and she wasn't in the mood for cat-and-mouse at this time of morning.

"Come on, Ric, stop playing games. My head can't take it right now."

She rolled onto her back and stared up at the cold hotel ceiling. A thousand things raced through her mind as to what her next story would be. She could cover the next governor's election and point out the pros and cons of each candidate. Or she could end up writing about the different conveniences in popup campers. Neither idea appealed to her much. She held out for a homicide.

"You, my dear, are going on tour with the Universal Wrestling World."

"The *what*?" she exclaimed.

Khristen forgot about the throbbing pain in her head. The last thing she wanted to do was travel around with those so-called athletes. Football and baseball players were athletes; she saw the pro wrestlers as nothing more than highly paid performers, actors who followed a script each and every night. No surprises there. And she'd seen only one event.

"The UWW. Forces beyond our control have beamed down some new assignments. Yours happens to be more of this wrestling stuff," he explained.

"Why me? Why do I have to do this sports junk? Surely Todd or Bret could handle this, couldn't they?"

This can only get better, but I'm not counting on it. Not from the tone of his voice. 'Be careful what you wish for,' as they say.

"Either one would give their left nut for a chance at this one. But they know the fight game all too well. The magazine wants a fresh look from a newcomer. So, lady, the job's all yours. A life of being on the road with 'The Flame.'"

"Please tell me you're not serious. I appreciate the chance to prove myself, but you have to know I don't know a thing about this wrestling stuff, Ric. The last thing I want to do is travel around with those guys after seeing them in action for one night. That was plenty for a life time, believe me."

"But just think, you'll be behind the scenes. You'll get to see the sweat stream out of their pores. Hear planned revenges. Smell and experience something most women would die for," he coaxed.

"I'm not most women, so cut the crap. I suppose I don't have a choice, do I?" She rolled over, giving in to her close friend and boss.

"Nope. You've been hinting about being a reporter for the last six months, Khristen. Here's your chance. It might not come again."

Khristen let out a long, drawn-out sigh. She raised her eyes to the ceiling, searching the heavens for some guidance, only to find none there for her to draw from. She'd have to accept this, now that she had the basis for the story on paper. It couldn't be so hard to continue with it. She may even be at an advantage, being a woman.

"Okay...what's the deal?"

She heard Ric shuffle through some papers and knew he was going to confirm whatever he had to tell her. Either that, or he was nervous and was searching for a way to share the details. She'd seen him do it in the past with the other writers, just before he handed out an assignment no one else volunteered for.

"You've got to be in Cedar Rapids on June fifth. That's next week, by the way. Ask for a Tommy Wilder. He'll give you all the information you need. The plane ticket and hotel info will be on your desk. Don't forget to pick them up when you drop off the piece."

"Cedar Rapids. June fifth."

"Yes. And Khristen..."

"What?"

"Be careful, but have fun. Come back with a good story."

"One more thing before you hang up," she said.

"Shoot."

"How long am I on this 'tour,' as you call it?"

"Six weeks, maybe six months... Until things change, I guess."

"Six months. Oh, God, please keep me sane."

She hung up the phone and glanced over the notes she had written.

Cedar Rapids. On tour. Like I really want to travel around with professional wrestlers.

She'd make the best of it and do her job. This was her chance to show Ric she could play with the big boys on the magazine's writing staff, that even without the credentials, she could do just as well as the rest of them…even if she wasn't fond of the assignment.

The room filled with the clicking sounds of a keyboard as fingers typed out the remaining few paragraphs of her first professional article on a sport she knew nothing about but had a feeling she would learn all too quickly.

* * * *

Beads of sweat had formed on Ric's brow when he hung up the phone. His deep-blue eyes conveyed a look of concern unlike any Shadoe had ever seen in them. If he didn't know better, he'd swear Ric Scott was in love with her—an emotion he had no time for or wanted interfering in his business.

Ric finished straightening out the pile of papers on his desk and glared at him square in the eye, not flinching for a second. Maybe he'd misjudged Scott, and he was made from the salt of the earth, after all.

"You know I hate doing this." Ric ran his fingers through short, dark hair. "You may own this magazine now, but that doesn't give you the right to play with people's lives just because you can."

Shadoe crossed the room, checking his rising

anger. "You're pretty gutsy for a guy who can be taken off the payroll at any time, Scott. Never mind the fact you were the one to recommend Khristen for the job, experienced or not. The fact that I do own this magazine does give me the right to alter people's jobs as I see fit. Having second thoughts?"

"Hey, what have I got to lose here? It's a job—one I love, but still only a job." Ric shoved papers across his desk. "Khristen, on the other hand…well, it's all she's wanted since coming here. I've seen her struggle with asking for a chance and being afraid to. You've just been the means to the end for her. I just hope she blows you out of the water with what she finds out. Whether you like it or not!"

Just what I like to see in my companies—people with balls.

Shadoe sat back in the overstuffed office chair. Before him sat a man who backed up his people, who believed in their abilities, a rare and beautiful characteristic not easily found these days—one his father had carried his entire life, in and out of the ring.

"And…I happen to care what becomes of her," Ric continued. "She's been a great asset to us, and we all love her very much. It's just not fair that she's being tricked like this."

"Tricked? She's not being tricked. It's a series of circumstances that gave her what she wanted. Granted, I've become fond of her, as well. I don't want how I feel to interfere with her judgment on the article."

"Great, but what do you gain from it? How do you benefit in the whole matter?" Ric asked.

"I get what could be a good reporter, an honest one I might add. And a little publicity doesn't hurt, either."

Not to mention a woman I'm starting to get crazy about.

"I get a story that lets people know more about the wrestling business—that not every man or woman who competes is a clown working in a circus tent."

"Don't you think when she finds out you gave her this dream come true, she'll be totally pissed off? Have you thought about her credibility when your association finally comes to surface? I'd bet my prized baseball card collection you haven't," Ric warned.

"To answer your questions...yes. Yes, I have given both areas deep thought. If she's got the character I think she has, there's no doubt in my mind she'll survive and land standing straight and tall. After that, we'll see what happens."

"Damn it, Donovan. She's not one of your playthings to just toss aside until the next time you're in town."

"You're out of line here, Scott!" Shadoe warned. "And beginning to walk on thin ice."

"I don't give a rat's ass if I am or not."

"Fine. Then sit your ass down and listen to me. First of all, she wouldn't be doing what she's doing if she was just a toy. I wouldn't have given her the time of day if she came across as being just that. Someone for me to take pleasure from until the next time, if there even was a next time. For Christ's sake, she doesn't even know who I am. I've managed to keep that from her and with your help, will continue to."

"Donovan, you've bitten off a little too much. I know her. She doesn't take to deception very well. You're looking for a test of character. Buddy, you're going to find it unless you 'fess up,' and it better be soon."

"I realize that," Shadoe said. "Speaking of character, I like yours. A man who's not afraid to get his own throat cut. The previous owner didn't give me any BS about you."

"Thanks, Donovan. Mark my words, though, if you even so much as cause a tear to drop from her eye, I'll bounce you off the wall."

"Well, that remains to be seen. However, there is something that needs to be taken care of. The receptionist, Susan, she's got to go. I deal with enough airheads nightly. I don't tolerate them in my businesses."

"I'll take care of it today. Now, what about Khristen?"

"She'll know soon enough. Just be prepared for the storm you're so convinced is going to hit. Remember to keep this between us, or else."

"Or else what?"

"Or else you'll be sharing the reception area with Susan's replacement."

"You do know how to threaten people."

"Yup, years of experience." Shadoe leaned over the desk and glared right into Ric's eyes. "Just don't forget who you work for and all that entails."

CHAPTER 6

Khristen arrived at an arena clogged with semi-trucks bearing the logo of the Universal Wrestling World. Men and women scurried around like squirrels gathering their nuts. Strewn on the pavement were dozens of black cables leading to and from the remote camera crews and slithering under a set of steel garage doors.

Khristen took a deep breath to calm her quaking nerves before stepping over the snake-like wires to reach someone who seemed to be in charge. She sucked in a breath of courage and tapped a burly man on a shoulder wider than the state of Montana.

"Excuse me, could you tell me where I might find Tommy Wilder?" Khristen nervously adjusted her briefcase strap.

The man turned and raked his gaze over her as if she were no one of importance. His inspection paused at the press pass hanging from her hip long enough to read it. Then he turned back to running the television cables to a semi-truck.

"Yeah, sure. Go through the doors, turn left, down the hall, second door on the right."

Khristen dismissed his scrutiny and followed the path he verbally mapped out for her. Anticipation grew as she witnessed muscle-bound men working feverishly on the ring. The men stretched and attached the canvas across the steel ring frame from corner to corner. They tested for its tightness and security before attaching the ring apron.

She meandered down an empty hall, stopped, and took a moment to calm herself one last time before stepping through a dressing room door.

"Is there..." The words caught in her throat. Khristen's free hand immediately covered her face, which grew warmer by the second. "Shit!"

Like a frightened girl watching a 1950's horror movie, Khristen couldn't fight the impulse to peek through her fingers. She was amazed her presence hadn't stopped the activities of the half-naked men. She felt all the more foolish when she realized these guys were more interested in the blackboard then a woman in their locker room.

Khristen brought her hand down and focused her eyes on the firm butts facing her. Some were covered in various colors, while others were either framed by jock straps or bare altogether. Whichever it was, a lot of muscles were flexing before her eyes. A quick and natural surge of lust sprang through her body. Maybe this assignment wasn't as bad as she first thought, but she doubted it.

"May I help you?"

"Huh?" The word stumbled out as her gaze traveled from head-to-toe of a man dressed in feathers. "Tommy Wilder. I was told I could find him here. Is he..." She had all she could do to fight the smirk about to play on her lips.

If they all wear costumes like this one, it's no wonder people think pro wrestling is a circus.

"Hey, T.W.!" the half-man, half-bird screeched. "Someone here to see ya."

Khristen watched as a tall, dark-haired man made his way through the others. Even though his six-foot, two-inch frame was lanky in comparison, he demanded and got respect from those around him; the men naturally parted for him much like the Red Sea for Moses.

"You must be Khristen Roberts," he said in an accent she couldn't place. He extended a hand that shook hers firmly. It was then she got a clear shot of what was holding the others' attention on the blackboard.

"Yes," she said.

Khristen's attention left the cartoons on the chalkboard to meet the man who'd be taking care of her. There wasn't a soft thing about him; he had the look of a Marine drill sergeant reviewing a new recruit in boot camp. She could see him already figuring out how best to get her to buckle under pressure.

"Those are very good," she said, smiling as she motioned to the cartoon characterizations drawing the men's attention.

"That's to let everyone know he's here," he

stated with a huff.

"Who's he?" she asked.

"Flame. He can't stand to see an empty chalkboard. Just a way for him to relax, I guess. Always seems to pick on someone. Good thing everyone laughs about it...sometimes all the way to the ring."

Wilder stopped briefly. A smug smile cornered the edges of his mouth. "I thought they would've sent a man."

"Are you saying a woman can't handle all this?" She waved her hand toward the men, who had finally realized a woman was in the room. They began to move in closer for a better look. This assignment was going to make her touchier than normal; she could feel it. Especially when a man who seemed light years behind the times would be her guide.

"No, what I'm saying is since you'll be traveling with us, maybe a man would've been better suited. Nothin' against you." Wilder took a deep breath and led her away from the locker room. "I'm sorry. There're a lot of men in this group, and I need their minds on the ring, not another pretty face. God knows there's enough tail floating around in each and every arena to take care of their needs. A different face every night is one thing, but a familiar woman is quite another."

His gaze swept past her shoulder in scrutiny. Khristen turned and followed it to the women standing in the hallway. She surveyed the "ladies" along the wall, getting his meaning. Groupies lingered in every corner, waiting for their chance to

RINGS OF PARADISE

pounce and hopefully capture their prey.

"These aren't all women wrestlers, are they?" she asked, knowing the answer all too well. She wanted confirmation that her observation of Wilder and the ladies were right on the head. These ladies had the "come hither" look in every aspect of their bodies.

"No. Maybe a few of them are. Women wrestlers had been a thing of the past, so we're rebuilding that aspect of the business. The men are still a bigger draw these days. Fantasy lovers for women and the bodies the local boys wish they had."

With curiosity, Khristen followed the direction of his slight nod and the look of disgust that came to rest on a thin young woman who Khristen guessed to be in her early twenties. The woman was dressed in slick black leather pants and matching four-inch spiked boots, and Khristen quickly got the gist of Wilder's meaning.

"Who's she?"

"She calls herself 'Cadillac.' Thinks she runs the whole show. Some of the guys just can't shake her. Like a bad penny, she keeps turning up," he said.

Khristen made a mental note of the groupie, thinking there'd be a place for someone of her...stature...somewhere in her article. She'd heard rock stars had groupies, yet it astounded her to find any woman on the planet would want to chase those sweaty bodies around.

I guess there's no limit on female desire.

She watched the woman shift gears into first

and make a run for one of the younger male wrestlers.

"Ms. Roberts?" Wilder called.

He didn't bother to turn in her direction, giving her no choice but to follow him into the seating area. She checked her watch and made a mental note of how much time she'd have before the matches began. Only three hours to go, and she still hadn't landed an interview with Flame, or any other wrestler, for that matter. Judging from Wilder's comments on the chalkboard art, Flame liked to be left alone before the matches. She'd honor that, but afterward, she'd seek him out.

"It's going to get pretty hectic from here on in. What do you want to see first?"

Khristen's enthusiasm and anticipation built as the crews continued to work on constructing the ring area. The floor mats were laid on top of more recording cable, and the announcer's booth construction looked to be nearly complete.

"Well, this is where it seems to begin. Might as well start here." Khristen set her oversized bag down taking a note pad and pencil from it.

"Good. There's a little more to it than just this. I'll be back sometime before the opening bell to take you to your seat."

With that in mind, Khristen smiled, watching the lanky middle-aged man walk away. He certainly did believe he was something, the way he strutted away from her.

Wilder turned back and looked straight into Khristen's eyes, making her feel that his next words were meant to be taken neither lightly, nor as an insult. "This is a man's sport. A one-on-one affair. Only the best and strongest survive," he said. He was like a mother hen protecting his little flock of chicks, or in this case, prized fighting cocks.

He'd issued her a warning of sorts. Well, she didn't take to that type of warning too lightly. If anything, she moved straight toward the subject of the warning, not away from it.

An affair, huh? Not the kind of an affair I'd want to play a part in! What kind of person does he think he's dealing with here?

She'd meet part of his challenge head-on just to prove a point.

Khristen flipped her notebook open and jotted down some notes. The frustration from Wilder's last comment seethed through her veins and came out at the tip of her pencil. The lead melted away on the paper from the heat of her frustration and smoldering anger.

She'd begun to dislike this assignment even more than she had the first morning Ric'd told her about it. She'd have to deal with a Neanderthal man like Wilder from here on in. Nothing in the world could make it go any easier, except maybe being pulled from this ridiculous story.

A man's world. Really, don't they know this is a new century?

Khristen felt aggravation build more as Wilder's words mixed with her own thoughts and ideas. In short phrases, she wrote about the harsh, and maybe true, words he'd spat out at her. The man definitely thought he was king of the hen house; if she wasn't careful, her words would reflect her thoughts and possibly jeopardize her story.

"Cock of the walk. Mmm, sounds dramatic to me."

Khristen froze at the sound of the all-too-familiar deep, sensual, soft voice. Swallowing hard, she turned to look at him leaning over her shoulder. Hot surprise radiated through her core, pinching the tip of her womanhood with a prickly hardness.

"Shadoe! What on earth?" she cried.

Here he was, live and in color, always knowing when she needed him to lift her spirits, to give her a break when it was most important that she have one. He never ceased to amaze her.

"I happened to flip on the TV the other night, caught some of this, and decided what the hell. I'm going to be in town, why not check it out? So, here I am."

She felt his eyes soak in every curve, every twinge her body made. The bluntness of his gaze made her body flush with sexual heat that moistened her panties to near embarrassment.

"But how'd you get in so early? The matches don't start for another hour or so."

She knew he had connections, but how did he always manage to show up wherever she was? Shadoe must have read her mind, because Khristen could see the color drain slowing from his face. Something was about to happen, and it didn't give her a warm and cozy feeling. Alarm sped through her.

"Khristen, there's something—"

"Mr. Donovan, if you please." Wilder's voice

echoed through the cave-like arena.

Shadoe's eyes pled for Khristen not to ask any more questions.

"I've got to go. Listen, I'll see you after you're done here. Okay?" he asked.

"Sure."

"Great."

He gave her a quick kiss on the cheek and bounded down the steps, heading toward an impatient Tommy Wilder. He disappeared toward the locker room area with Wilder close behind.

Now what in blazes is going on?

She couldn't make out what was being said, but it looked as if the two were having a few unfriendly words.

* * * *

"How do you know her, Donovan?" Wilder accused. "She's not one of your playmates, is she?"

"You're out of line here!" Shadoe spat, fighting to hold his temper in check. He didn't want to defend Khristen too much—especially not with Tommy Wilder, the one man who could make his wrestling career a living hell if he chose to do so. He'd seen it happen too many times—men's and women's careers destroyed simply because they didn't agree to go along with the script.

"Am I? I believe with the rumors about your adventures with the ladies, it gives me every right to ask how you know her. After all, she seems to be innocent, not the type you're usually with," Wilder said.

Shadoe stopped, grabbing Wilder by the arm.

"You know, Wilder, if you listen hard enough

to the locker room conversations, you may be a little surprised to hear your escapades brought up from time to time. As for my knowing the lady, I do. You might even say I hold her future right here, tight in my fist. A fist, I might add, that will connect with your mouth if you say one more indecent insinuation about Khristen."

Well, so much for holding back my temper. Damn! I can't stop here defending her, or he'll just keep prodding.

His body trembled with anger. He had to calm down and get his mind back on the ring and what he had left to do tonight; face another opponent hell-bent on claiming his championship belt.

Wilder turned, coming toe-to-toe with Shadoe. "A first-name basis. I had no idea she meant that much to you. Am I to believe a woman has actually caught the soul of Shadoe Donovan? Or is the heart of your sexual conquests involved here?"

Wilder pulled out of his grasp and walked toward the locker rooms with Shadoe not a half step behind.

"She's caught something she didn't even know she wanted, or needed. As for that heart, it's under wraps and will remain so. This one's not a prize to be won; she's a woman to be cherished," Shadoe stated, defending Khristen's honor.

"Just as long as it doesn't affect your performance, and it's kept at a minimum. Because I'll tell you here and now, if it does have an effect, I don't care what strings I have to pull, you'll be on a medical recoup for an indefinite amount of time." Wilder marched back down the hall toward the arena.

"Your threats are empty, Wilder. About as empty as the arenas will be without Flame out there jacking up the ticket sales. I don't think that's a chance you or the federation is willing to take," Shadoe disputed, half-believing his own words.

* * * *

Even though Shadoe had never told her exactly what his job was, Khristen remembered it had something to do with public relations. Could it be possible his company, whatever it was, would be doing something with the UWW? Maybe he'd even asked to be specifically assigned to the account in hopes of seeing her.

It's possible, isn't it? Heck, she didn't know, and she really didn't care. Well, maybe she did care...a lot. Anyway, all that mattered was she'd see him at the end of the night.

She'd found it hard to keep her mind on anything more than Shadoe. Day and night, she dreamt of him, whether it was shopping at the mall or sitting in a fast food joint, he was imbedded in her soul.

"Ms. Roberts?"

Wilder's voice pierced into her deep concentration, causing her to jump.

"What? Yes?"

"It's time for you to get seated."

"Okay."

Khristen gathered her belongings in a rush of anticipation and followed Wilder down a makeshift pathway. Steel railings lining the cement path were designed to keep the screaming and grabbing fans from getting too close to their heroes and villains. What seemed like several moments in reality had been less than a minute when they entered the square area surrounding the ring. The steel railings continued their trail, separating UWW personnel from the paying audience.

Wilder introduced Khristen to the timekeeper and ring announcer; then handed her an official laminated UWW press pass and gave her arm a quick squeeze. She could see by the look in his eye it was his way of telling her to watch out, to keep attentive of the situation around her at all times. She felt sure he didn't want to be attending to a hapless female journalist.

Khristen clipped the second press pass to her belt, wondering how all these people had gotten past her. She then realized that even though she'd been sitting near the dressing rooms, she hadn't noticed people were slowly filtering in.

Sitting in the center of thousands of people around and above her in the seats climbing the sloping sides, Khristen felt like a goldfish in a bowl. An awesome rush filled her to be the center of attention, if only for a fleeting moment.

The roar of the crowd echoed in Khristen's ears as the house lights dimmed, leaving only the hot flood lights above the ring burning blindly. The mounting excitement and the sound of a bell at ringside gave her goose bumps causing the hair on her arms to stand at attention. The excitement was like a plague; it infected every single person in the arena, including her.

"If you have any questions, please be sure to

RINGS OF PARADISE

ask. No matter how rough it looks out there, these guys are trained professionals." The tuxedo-clad ring announcer placed a reassuring hand on her shoulder. His mouth curled into a warm smile under a graying mustache. "They're trained to fall and to take the punches. It protects them as much as their opponents."

"What about the feuds? If I recall, they can get pretty intense," she said. Khristen's concern for her own safety rang in her words as she tried to maintain a little self-respect for the sake of her long-dreamed-of career. She didn't want her companions to believe she was ignorant or frightened, even if she was.

Never let them see you sweat!

"Yeah, some do. Hell, most of these guys travel together. But once they're in the ring, it's all business. Family ties and friendships are put aside."

"Family?"

"Wrestling is sometimes a family tradition. In some cases, it can pit brother-in-law against brother-in-law, but very rarely brother against brother. Although…there's always a first time. For some of the guys, it's a way of life they grew up with—one that can end their life before it even begins. A few have left us never knowing what it felt like to be forty, or to see their children graduate from high school."

The announcer flashed a quick wink and then climbed into the ring. He held a microphone in one hand and a list of the competitors in the other. The roar of the crowd grew louder, and the bell rang out twice more. Things were about to get interesting from here on in.

"Welcome wrestling fans!" he bellowed into the mic with all the enthusiasm and excitement of a long-time veteran.

Khristen listened and watched the crowd's reaction as the announcer made his initial introductions and pushed some of the merchandise available in the lobby. The standard warnings were issued about city ordinances on smoking and misconduct and the consequences of violating them.

The roar behind her grew louder when one of the many cameras swung in its direction. Everyone wanted to be on TV. Everyone wanted to be the rowdiest. Everyone was crazy in Khristen's opinion.

The bell rang out again to signal the first two competitors to make their way to the ring.

"Tell me about these two guys," she shouted, leaning closer to her ringside companions to hear them over the music and crowd. The noise was near deafening.

"These guys are okay. See the one with the big gold gem-studded dollar sign on his belt? He's an arrogant son-of-a-buck. Thinks money is the answer to everything," the bell keeper stated, covering his table mic with a free hand.

Khristen looked over the ruggedly handsome face and well-muscled body. Each hair was in place; his attire, freshly pressed linen.

"If he's so rich, why does he do this for a living? Surely he doesn't make all his money beating up people in public," she said.

"No one knows for sure where it comes from. It's just there, and believe you me, he flaunts it as much as possible," one of the TV announcers said.

"Mmm. What about the other one?"

She knew the answer as the words came from her mouth. Inexperience radiated off him like the light of a neon sign in the dark of night.

"A rookie. This is basically a warm-up match."

Khristen nodded and continued to watch in silence as The Money Man strutted around the ring, showing off his belt and supposedly authentic gem-studded tear-away silver-blue tuxedo.

As soon as the bell rang, the rookie flew at his opponent, only to make a connection with a waiting turnbuckle. Before he had time to turn around, Money Man swept him into a headlock and twisted his neck until Khristen thought for sure it would pop off. The young recruit gave a shove at the smoothly sculpted body and escaped...for a moment.

The match came to an end within ten minutes as did the next few matches, which came and went without incident. Khristen's fingers, moist with sweat, allowed the pencil to slip around in them whenever she made some key notations. Next time, she would bring a tape recorder with her.

Hopefully, there won't be a next time.

On more than one occasion, she voiced an opinion along with thousands of paying fans. Each time she protested, she felt a warm rush of embarrassment and fumbled with the note pad, smiling shyly at the timekeeper.

"The man of the hour is next, Ms. Roberts. The wrestler I'm told you'll be traveling with. Here." Wilder offered her a folded piece of paper.

"What's this?" Khristen took the paper into her possession.

"Beats me. I was asked to be the delivery boy, not recite it to you."

Khristen unfolded the paper, carefully reading the written words over several times.

No matter what you see tonight, remember I am the man you know. The man who showed you what paradise is all about and gave you everything on that trip.

Khristen's fingers shook as she folded the note along its creases.

"Some joke, Wilder, only I'm not laughing." Khristen wanted to punch him but instead crushed the note in her tight fist.

"Now listen here, little lady! I have no idea what this is all about, and I don't care. Your affairs are yours personally. Just don't let them interfere with what goes on in the ring. *Capiche*?" said Wilder as he took his leave of her.

"And what, if I may ask, are you referring to here? I don't know who would send me this. Or is it just a sick ploy on your part, hoping I'd go running off like some flustered little school girl?" she yelled at his backside, wishing she could plant the palm of her hand across his face.

Her words snapped out of her mouth with a controlled snootiness. She didn't recognize the person inside her any more. Anger made her voice tremble. Her ringside companions looked at her as if she were a mad woman. She turned away, embarrassed by her unprofessional outburst.

The cheers from the crowd drew Khristen's

attention back to the ring at the entrance of the birdman she'd encountered earlier. The roar intensified when he went from corner to corner flapping his arms as if takeoff was inevitable. Khristen chuckled to herself at his antics, trying to forget her annoyance with Wilder and the note.

The thunder of heart-pounding music echoed deeply in the arena. Hundreds of boos fought hard to be heard above the music.

Khristen felt the drumbeat vibrate deep in her heart and soul, echoing through every cavern in her body, bouncing from wall to wall. She found she had no control. The excited anticipation igniting in her started with a tingling sensation in her head and ended with the twitching muscles in her entire body. Her body answered the call of the sexual, seductive music that crawled in a slow wave up her spine.

A sea of arms moved toward the ring as the object of the catcalls pushed its way through the wave. Khristen stood and strained to see the man who would soon be passing within just a few feet of her. Finally, she'd see the one wrestler everyone seemed to love to hate—Flame.

He hit the ring with all the arrogance of a cocky, streetwise kid. Hair slicked back to a curly, dark, shiny gleam. Mirrored glasses covered his eyes. Head cocked to one side, a sneer prominent on his lips, he nonchalantly looked over his worthy opponent.

His cocky strut took him to Khristen's side of the ring. With a flick of a finger, he snapped the glasses off and tossed them with precise direction. Their eyes met—one set with a quick and piercing plea for understanding, the other pair filling with tears caused by confusion, anger, and a sense of betrayal.

Khristen picked the glasses from her lap, the warmth of Flame's face still lingering on them. It took all her strength and dignity not to throw them back; straight back at a man she'd thought she could trust. A man she thought of as her friend. The man she fought so hard not to desire but found impossible not to. He'd made her believe in little girl dreams of the white knight in shining armor again. The man who made a small piece of paradise nothing without him by her side.

The man who just shattered my life with the simple flick of a finger.

Shadoe!

The bell rang out, and the match began when the bird-like man delivered a forearm smash to the back of Flame's neck. Khristen cringed at the transformation taking place in Shadoe's eyes. The savagery of Flame she never would've guessed to be a side of Shadoe's calm and loving manner quickly took hold of him. Flame turned and glared at his opponent like a bull ready to charge. Khristen visualized smoke coming out of his nostrils as his body grew tense and stiff. His well-muscled body swelled and came alive.

In a flash, like lightning across a stormy sky, Flame bounced off the ropes, drove his rigid body in fluid motion to the other side of the ring, and delivered a patent clothesline that flattened his adversary with such force, Khristen heard the flesh smack solidly against the tightly drawn canvas.

RINGS OF PARADISE

Flame pulled his stunned victim off the mat with a handful of hair and then delivered a chop across the withering man's throat area that once again laid him flat. He stepped on his opponent as if he were a throw rug. Flame paraded around the ring as the crowd's jeers mixed loudly with fewer cheers.

"This can't be Shadoe. I can't believe he'd do this...not my Shadoe!" she said more to herself than anyone around her. She looked on with mixed feelings at the change that had come over him.

"Ms. Roberts, are you okay?"

"Whoa, she's white as a ghost. Here, have 'er drink this."

The ring announcer handed a fresh glass of water to the timekeeper.

"Ms. Roberts?" The timekeeper placed a Styrofoam cup in her hand.

Khristen brought it to her lips, taking a sip of the cool water, and stared at Flame. No amount of moisture could begin to put out the burning fear and anger in the pit of her stomach.

Flame backed up onto the top rope, cocked an elbow skyward, and then sprang high into the air to connect with a flying elbow smash to the head. His opponent bounded up into a sitting position before falling semi-conscious back onto the canvas. Flame covered his man, the referee leaped down onto the mat and slapped out a three-count on the canvas. Declared the victor, Flame stood in the center of the ring, hand and belt raised in the air.

He exchanged a few niceties with some of the spectators at ringside, stepped through the ropes, and then hopped down in front of Khristen. Without further hesitation, he flashed her a quick and loving smile, showing for a brief moment the real him...Shadoe. Then Flame waded back through the same sea of arms that had greeted him only moments before.

Khristen's fingers trembled as she tried to hold onto the pencil, paper, and the silver glasses. Her mind spun in a hundred different directions. Confusion clouded her reason. She heard her own voice softly excuse herself from the table. Her legs seemed to have minds of their own as they carried her back to the dressing room area.

In the wake of Flame's departure, Khristen burst through the locker room door without taking notice of a few naked men.

She had one thing—one person—in mind.

"Khristen!"

Khristen turned in a flurry at the sound of her name. Sweat ran down his face and into his eyes. His long hair hung in drenched curls. Damn, if he didn't look good enough to eat if she wasn't so angry with him.

"Public relations! Knows almost nothing about the sport! Right," she said.

She flung the glasses at him and then left the sweaty locker room not knowing who called out her name—Flame, or Shadoe.

CHAPTER 7

"Khristen!" His voice bounced off the hallway walls like a sonic boom.

Her pace quickened to a full jog. Khristen pushed and slammed open a service door with such impact, it rang through the hall like the clank of heavy chains being dropped. His hand grabbed onto her arm just before she made it to the edge of the parking lot. The sound of her hand meeting his cheek rang out as he swung her around into his arms.

"Let go of me, you bastard! You lied to me. All this time you've been lying," she hissed.

"I had to; don't you see?"

"No! You must have had a good laugh or two at my expense." She struggled in his grip, but he wouldn't let her go. "How stupid I must have seemed whenever we talked about this assignment."

"Will you shut up and listen for once in your life, you little nit? I was protecting—"

"Who? Me? I don't see it. The only person you were protecting was yourself. All that talk of honesty, friendship, trust. Yeah, right. What a joke I must have been in the locker room."

Shadoe covered Khristen's trembling lips with his own before she could utter another word. He coaxed the anger from her, his tongue being the carrot dangled in front of that hostility. Her rigid body relaxed under the desire caused by the sweet sensation of the moist probe artfully toying with hers.

He pulled her closer to him; the struggle to escape ended. The heat of him sweet, Shadoe held her body at his command; the feral Flame long gone.

He held her close in his arms. "Go home, Khristen. Go home and sleep. Things will look different in the morning, after you've come to your senses," he whispered.

"After I've come to my senses?" The anger not yet put fully to rest resurfaced. Her body grew ridged in his arms.

She pulled away from him. Coldness quickly filled the void.

"How unlike you, Shadoe, to leave me here after what just happened," she said. "After seducing me into a false sense of trust since we first met. That's a price you'll never be able to repay. Never in a million years, my friend."

"Well, honey, if that's the way it's got to be this time around, then so be it. You're angry, and I'm in no mood to deal with an irate woman right now. Just do as I ask, Khristen. Go home, take a cold shower, and cool off."

Shadoe abandoned her in the vast lot and called back as he headed toward the door, "I'll talk to you later. You can bet on that."

* * * *

The night turned out to be a hellish one. Khristen sat in her hotel room attempting to pump out the article, only to find her mind overwhelmed with visions of Shadoe fading into Flame. Visions of him entering the ring invaded her judgment every time she tried to write objectively. The whole thing became more and more unbelievable.

How'd he manage to hide such an important piece of information? Damn!

He's a master of deception. After all, it's what he does for a living night after night. Even when he held me close and kissed me so sweetly, he must have been hatching his moves.

A part of her refused to believe it. Her heart pleaded for her to believe in him, while her mind and damaged soul refused to let reason take hold. She didn't take kindly to lies, and he had a garbage bag full of them.

After all the time they'd spent together, sharing their hopes and fears…

Not once did he hint at being a wrestler. Not once did he trust me enough to tell me the truth.

It did explain his presence at each event and his nervousness when she talked about Flame. Here she'd thought he was a little jealous. If truth be told, she'd hoped it was jealousy.

Confusion and anger replaced any concentration she could halfheartedly muster. She realized this part of the report was lost; she'd have to rely on her notes in the morning. She'd much rather hide away in bed far from the real world, far away from continuing to care for a man she loved.

Several hours passed before she slid in between the cold white sheets and fell into an uneasy sleep. Dreams of Shadoe's loving and caring eyes caressing her melted into the fierceness of Flame's bloodthirsty look, sending her tossing and turning across her queen size bed.

Shadoe's kisses covered her throat, and his fingertips tweaked her nipples. He drove her further and further into that place every women dreams of—a place where she is conquered by her prince.

When she looked into his eyes, it was Flame who claimed her with his body, Flame who took from her what she'd meant to be Shadoe's. Deep inside, her body screamed for the monster to release her, but he wouldn't. He only sneered at her, laughing as her body betrayed her.

Khristen woke with a start, her hair damp from perspiration, as the sun peeked over the tops of the curtains. The sheet and blanket were twisted around her legs, and her nightgown felt clammy against her skin. She shivered as she climbed out of bed.

Standing in front of the bathroom mirror, she splashed cold water on her face before taking a long look at her reflection. There was a slight grayness evident under her eyes. The once-tamed ponytail looked like a rat's nest. Her good night's sleep had disappeared somewhere between the man she trusted and the one who betrayed that trust.

Stepping into the shower, she welcomed the hot

water pelting on her body. She wanted nothing more than to beat out the agitation and go over the previous evening with a rational mind.

By her recollection, it all appeared clear up until the time when Shadoe, or rather Flame, came to the ring. That's when the haze started to set in, become denser with confusion.

The way Flame strutted to the ring, the glasses he tossed on my lap, the savage look in his eye.

She remembered she'd followed him back to the locker room, Shadoe calling her name, and she yelling something at him about public relations, and then throwing those silver glasses back at him. Nothing, yet everything, seemed to have changed with that incident.

He'd betrayed her, plain and simple. That betrayal of her trust cut deeper than anything any other person could've done to her. She'd rather he'd just used her body for his pleasure as Dane had.

She would never trust his word again. How could she? If a person could not trust a friend, a best friend, who could they trust?

She rinsed her hair and then shut off the shower.

"It's morning, and things don't look any different, Shadoe."

Wrapped in an oversized towel, Khristen poured herself some hot tea. She opened the morning paper, going straight to the sports section, and searched for any news on the previous night's matches, finding nothing.

No surprise there. A professional wrestling match would never make the paper. Not unless a competitor died in the ring, or there was some sort of drug scandal. Only then would the sport be newsworthy.

"There's got to be an explanation for all this. How did he manage to... Who's there?" she asked of the pounding on her hotel room door. "And why should I care anyway?"

"Delivery, madam."

"Just a minute, please."

Khristen checked to make sure the tie secured her robe before she pulled open the door.

"I didn't order—" she said.

In the hallway stood a young man fully dressed in the proper hotel attire, carrying a large bouquet full of exotic flowers. He had to look around them in order to see Khristen and make his way past her. He set the vase on the gleaming cherry wood tabletop and flashed a warm smile.

"No, no, no! I didn't order these! You must have the wrong room."

"You are Khristen Roberts, aren't you?"

"Why yes, but—" she argued.

"Then I have the right room. I'm only doing my job, ma'am." The bellboy turned to her as he walked out the door. "Enjoy your stay in Cedar Rapids."

Khristen pulled the card from its envelope. The casing contained only a single note card, with one word scrolled on it.

"Shadoe."

Despite herself, an amused smile seeped onto her face, and warmth enveloped her heart.

"Well, at least he's still persistent."

Breathtaking. That's what last night had been when Shadoe had kissed her like a bandit stealing precious time. When his lips met hers, even angry, she felt as if time had indeed stood still. Yet, it had moved on so quickly. Too quick for her. It had cut right through the anger she'd not been willing to let go of...but had.

It was beyond her control—something she'd have to learn to deal with and harness quickly.

"Cut it out, Khristen! Get a hold of yourself! This man is totally out of your league. He's no doubt got a woman in every city from here to China. Not to mention the fact that he's a lying, deceitful, overgrown bully." She scolded herself while trying to fight the feelings growing inside of her.

"Wait a minute here."

She stopped short in front of the flowers. They were exotic enough that she knew where they were native to.

Hawaii.

History seemed to be repeating itself.

Khristen's memory brought back the bittersweet moment that had occurred three months earlier. It had been the day he suggested going snorkeling and spending the day together, the day their passion and misgivings were swept out along with the tide. The subject of the magazine, the assignment, and his lack of knowledge about pro wrestling had been dropped so elegantly. He'd succeeded in the art of distraction that day in the sand.

"Help? Yeah, right. I wonder."

Picking up the phone, she dialed Ric Scott's office telephone number.

"*Plain Talk*. May I help you?"

"Ric Scott, please," she said.

"Ric, here."

"Ric, this is Khristen. Where's Susan?"

"I didn't want to have to share the reception area with her, so I let her go instead."

"What?"

"Never mind, long story. What's up?"

"I need you to do a couple of things for me."

"Sure, what are they? Get you a date with one of the grapplers you're hanging with these days?"

"Get real, will you? This is serious, Ric. Do you remember when I went to Hawaii a few months ago?"

"Yeah, like it was yesterday. That's when the news came down about the magazine," he said.

"Right. Has anything happened to shed some light on just who bought it? Like for instance, who signs the paychecks?"

She paced the room, waiting for Ric's reply. If only there was some clue that he could give to help her start putting some pieces together. Anything, no matter how small, would be of help.

"Nope, the money's direct deposited with a local payroll service. Remember, it was one of the stipulations of the buyer, along with your new position of course."

"What about company memos, letters, messages, anything like that which would indicate a name?"

Come on, there's got to be something!

RINGS OF PARADISE

"Strike number two. None of that is done in this office anymore. Want to try for strike three, and you're out?"

"Not yet. And Ric, this is just between you and me, okay?"

"Sure, but why?"

"No particular reason. Just keep it between the two of us, though."

"Are you sure everything's okay out there? Those guys are treating you okay, aren't they? I could try to get you off of this assignment, if only I knew who to contact."

"No, it's okay. Nothing I can't handle. I'll keep you posted, though. Thanks for the help. 'Bye."

She hung up the telephone with no more information than she'd had before the call. Now she'd have to ready herself for the next step of her journey—how to deal with Shadoe and the UWW.

"I can't be bribed into forgiveness, Mr. Donovan." Khristen took a long sniff of the fragrant flowers and then dropped them into the waste can.

* * * *

Shadoe came from the bathroom with nothing more than a towel on. With wet, soapy hands, he grabbed the ringing phone, knocking it to the floor.

"Damn!"

He bent to pick it up and grabbed the towel to keep it from slipping off completely. Not that there was anyone there who cared. He was completely alone, heart, body, and soul.

"Hello."

"What the hell is going on, Donovan?" The low growl came through the line sounding like something between an injured animal and one on the prowl.

"Excuse me, who is this?" Shadoe secured his loin covering.

"You heard me. Just what the hell is going on there?"

"Scott, is that you?"

"No, it's Fred Flintstone. Who do you think it is?"

"What's wrong with you, anyway?"

The last thing he needed right now was to deal with a man who obviously had something on his mind. Especially when he was still trying to figure out what he was going to do about Khristen, how he was going to make amends.

"Oh, nothing. The usual, everyday occurrence of a certain feature writer who called and asked some pretty weird questions about the magazine. Questions I've been sworn to secrecy about. Questions you were warned about from the very beginning."

Shadoe played dumb. "Are you talking about Khristen?"

"No, Florence Nightingale. Who the hell do you think? Of course Khristen!"

He should've known this would happen, that she'd call questioning the magazine. It was true, he'd been warned, but as usual, ignored those warnings, deciding his way was the only way— Attitude he attributed to the Irish in him, stubborn, unconsciously looking for a fight of wills.

His mama had told him to be careful, or he'd end up just like his dad. He didn't think that was so bad. It was how his parents became his parents—the fire of passion sparked by more than one stormy battle between them. Nope, he wasn't going to go down in defeat so easily. He'd just begun to fight the battle of wills with Khristen.

He wasn't used to losing, and he wasn't about to start now.

"Donovan, are you there?"

He ran a hand through his wet hair and sat lazily on the couch, forgetting he was dripping wet. He didn't care that the towel had since come unfastened and all that Mother Nature had given him was exposed to anyone who bothered to look. There wasn't any one here to take in the view he offered; he'd made sure of that last night.

"Yeah," he answered.

"So, what is happening," Ric asked.

"To put it mildly, she now knows what type of public relations I'm involved with," Shadoe said.

"Before or after the matches."

"During. Actually, when she saw me walk the runway to the ring. I've got to say one thing for her; she wallops a good slap," he chuckled.

"She hit you? Why, Khristen doesn't have a violent bone in her body. Some influence you are on her. You've managed to take a sweet, civil woman and turn her into a brawler like you," Ric accused.

"Cool it, Scott. I had it coming for hiding the truth from her. I just didn't expect—"

"Didn't expect? Did you really think she'd be passive and tell you it was okay that you lied to her? If I know her as well as I think I do, she probably called you every name in the book."

"Only one, and then I put her mouth to rest."

"You didn't."

"Oh, yes I did. A long, drawn out smacker she didn't stand a chance of resisting," Shadoe said. The thought of the kiss still made his loins burn, relighting a smoldering fire that flamed his manhood. He covered his lap with the wet towel, hoping to put the lion to sleep, at least for the time being.

"Oh, you kissed her." Ric sounded relieved.

"What else, you fool? You didn't think—"

"Hey, look at the profession you're in. Bouncing people around is almost a nightly thing for you."

"Is that what the public thinks after all the rotten publicity? That professional wrestlers are the same out of the ring as in?" Shadoe couldn't believe everyone who watched professional wrestling could possible think that they were just as violent outside the ring as inside.

The public couldn't be that blind. Or could they?

"The public believes what they read and see. All they see of wrestling is what's on TV and in magazines. The ring side of it, not the day-to-day living of the men and women who take all the punishment in the ring," Ric pointed out smugly.

"That's one of the reasons why I bought a magazine—to wake up the public regarding this business. Somehow, I feel the original issue has gotten sidetracked."

"Then give Khristen the other side of the coin. Get your heart to slow down, and show her what needs to be done to make it in your world."

"How could I be so sightless?" Shadoe looked blindly at his surroundings and ran his hand over his face in frustration. Scott was right and most likely knew it. Shadoe had let the business side of things slide while his body took over. He wouldn't make that mistake again.

"Because you're an egomaniac and see things through your heart not your head. It happens to the best of us, Donovan. That nasty 'L' word that scares men to hell."

"Love? Who said anything about love?" He sprang up from the couch and paced the floor as far as the phone cord would allow him to go. Ric Scott had to be mad to think love had anything to do with anything. Business was business, and what was going on between Khristen and himself was just that—business.

"You did by your actions. Later, Donovan."

Shadoe heard the click of the phone through his fog of confusion. Had he heard Scott correctly? Could that have been the dreaded "L" word that came out of his mouth? A cool shiver soared through him, warming when it reached his heart. His heart had been captured by a woman who wasn't afraid of him, who stood up to him, no matter what. Did he dare to believe that he could be in love with her? When had it all begin to matter to him?

When did she begin to matter?

If, through no fault but his own, Khristen always saw the ringside of things, he'd have to make some arrangements and fast. He'd have to somehow show her the behind-the-scenes strains of being a professional wrestler. He'd have to make her understand completely before he lost more than his championship belt.

CHAPTER 8

"Ms. Roberts, are you ready yet? The car is prepared to leave in ten minutes." The male voice informed her through the hardwood door of her hotel room.

"Okay, thanks." Khristen hurried across the room, packed the last of her belongings, and then headed out the door. With suitcase, laptop, and briefcase in hand, she pressed the down button with an elbow and struggled to keep from dropping everything when her purse slipped down her shoulder.

Six flights down, the elevator doors opened to the bustling lobby. Khristen allowed a bellboy to take her bags out to the white luxury sedan waiting just outside the lobby doors.

"I hope you weren't waiting too long." She slipped into the front seat.

"Only a lifetime since last night."

"Shadoe! Where's Wilder? I thought I'd be

riding in his car." She touched her cheek and wondered whether the slap from last night still stung his. Probably not near as much as her hand had. Just the thought of it made her palm throb.

This isn't good. Not good at all.

After slapping his face last night, this could only mean one thing. She was in for one heck of a ride if she had to stay here with him.

The engine purred, and Shadoe slipped the car into gear. The vehicle sped forward. The thought of jumping out crossed her mind; she'd do anything not to be this close to him. But, if she jumped out, there'd be serious injury to her body, and her pain threshold wasn't that high. She was stuck, plain and simple.

"I talked him into this arrangement instead. I also convinced him this would be strictly business. Aren't you supposed to get an up-close-and-personal look at Flame?" He glanced over at her, fire in his eyes.

Was that anger she heard in his voice, or contemplated revenge? By the look in his eye, she believed both. She was sure he'd mastered revenge to an art.

"Yes, but—"

"But nothing! Just remember what you've said from the start about this article." His voice soft, edged with strength, sent shivers down her spine. "I'm counting on you, Khristen, to be honest. No sugar coating, and no assumptions about pro wrestling."

"So then, betrayal is a part of this way of life. Convince the unsuspecting outsider that you're being honest and then deceive them," she snapped.

"Keep your personal views out of it, too," he warned.

She held her quivering nerves in check. The last thing she wanted was to lose control of her temper in the car with him. She really wanted to lash out at him; to remind him of what and who he really was—nothing more than a Casanova adding notches to his boots. A liar amongst all the men she knew.

"I'm me, and Flame is Flame. The first, a real, live, caring person. The second, an alter ego who'll do anything to keep the fans interested and the UWW contract signed."

His voice echoed inside the car somewhere between pleading for her to understand and wanting to shake that knowledge into her. If he was trying to scare her, it didn't work. Even if it had, she'd never let him know it.

"So who is driving this car? Shadoe the jerk, or Flame the bully? Whose voice do I hear? Who's lying, and who's not? Just who in the hell are you right now?"

She leaned on her door to get a better look at him, to see if he flinched with another lie.

"Who do you want me to be, Khristen? Being Flame is my chosen career. I was born and bred for this way of life; it's what I do best, and I love doing it. Nothing—and I repeat, nothing—is going to change that right now. Especially not some female writer hell-bent on stealing my heart and soul."

"Excuse me? Stealing your heart and soul? I think you've been pile-driven once too often if you think that. If I remember right, it was you who did the chasing. You're the one who's always been there when I've needed a shoulder—unexpectedly, I might add. But it's all clear now, since you and Flame are of the same body."

"That's right. The two share the same body, the same spirit, but not the same mind. We're as different as dry dirt and mud," he said. "One ingredient in common, but nothing else."

"Why did you outright lie to me, then?" she asked.

He better have a good answer, too. I'm not about to settle for some generic typical male response. Even if there's a remote possibility of it being the truth.

"Because when we met on the plane, I knew you were different. I thought that while I was there, it would be nice to spend some time with you. Is it my fault destiny threw us together? I don't want to be used for my assets, monetary or otherwise. I told you I was careful when it came to my profession, didn't I," he reminded her.

"Right, so you picked up a nice girl to show her what men are really about, only to confirm her beliefs that men are all the same. All of your species want to prove their manhood with conquests of the innocent," she responded, hoping to put a nail in his control.

Shadoe slammed his fist on the stirring wheel.

"Damn it, Khristen! That's not the way it is, and you damn well know it. If you were just a conquest, do you think you would've lasted this long? Not a chance. I care about you and your feelings."

"Words spoken in anger, Shadoe," she said. "You also said something about public relations. How does that fit in here? The only PR I see is the reaction of the audience toward you. In case you haven't noticed, it's not all that great, either. From my vantage point, there's more hate than love for Flame out there."

"Remember, you've been in only two arenas. Flame is caught between good and evil. For every voice who cried out against him last night, there's a matching one in his favor. That's the deal, the price we pay in this sport."

"Sport? You call beating up another person in front of hundreds, maybe thousands, of people a sport? Baseball, bowling, golf—those are sports. What you play is bully of the school yard," she said. "Go ahead, admit it. Be honest with yourself for once."

"Wrestling's a choreographed sport, that's all. We've all gone to one school or another to learn how to take the punches," he explained fruitlessly.

"Actors—just a bunch of actors."

Just as I thought, the skill without the pay.

"More like a stunt man. Time for your first lesson, sweetheart. You're about to get honest with your own ideals."

He turned into the driveway of a local health club, and shivers soared through her. The smug look returned to his face. His mouth was tight, and the coldness in his eye caused the shivers to plunge further into the deep freeze. No mistaking that kind of look—he was angry, and determined to teach her a thing or two. She prayed she'd survive to write about it.

"Come on. You'll see just what has to be done to act in the ring." He slammed the door and headed for the entrance, not giving her a second glance.

Khristen got out of the car and followed him into the facility. They stopped briefly at the front desk before continuing down the hallway to the locker room where he changed his clothes.

She waited for him to come out while some other UWW wrestlers passed by. Her curiosity rose after a number of them went into the open weight room. Shadoe grasped her arm, and she felt herself firmly being led past rows of assorted workout equipment, where he found an available lifting bench to begin his first routine. He laid on his back, hair spilling over the bench edge, and grasped a bar holding the two-hundred-and-fifty-pound weights.

Sweat beaded up while he slowly counted off the required repetitions. Lines grew deep in his face from the strain.

Khristen made note of each grunt and groan that forced its way from his throat. Each muscle grew with intensity, straining to break out from its casing. Shadoe seemed to forget her presence, concentrating solely on his body and the punishment he gave it. At one point after the first few repetition sets, Flame flickered briefly in his eye. She looked on with caution while the intensity of Flame combined with the passion of Shadoe until the two were one kindred spirit.

He moved over to another machine, adjusted the weights, and began another routine of leg lifts.

RINGS OF PARADISE

The padded bar rested on top of his foot and became the beginning point of the pressure his massive leg muscles took on. Under the tank shirt, his stomach muscles rippled and tightened with each lift. Calves and thighs grew stronger with each repetition.

Khristen followed him through the weight room. Her body tired and ached in sympathy at each piece of equipment and grueling routine Shadoe endured. Now she understood what he went through in order to keep in shape for the punishment he took in the ring.

Much like a prizefighter or an all-star linebacker, his body had to be in top condition. His mind had to be focused. His heart had to be consumed by the love of what he did nightly. All of those things were etched deep on his face.

Shadoe sat on the edge of another bench with legs on either side. His elbow rested inside his thigh with a fifteen-pound cold steel weight in his hand, and the repetition started up once again. His curly, damp hair hung slightly over his eyes; sweat trickled down the pumped-up biceps.

He looked at her through stringy, wet hair. His eyes and the curve of his mouth seemed to say, *"Had enough? Don't count on it. It's just the beginning."*

With a towel draped around his broad, damp shoulders, Shadoe stood and unbuckled the weight lifting belt. His hair dripped with sweat. His well-muscled body gleamed with moisture. The black tank shirt clung to every crevice in his chest.

Khristen felt the familiar desire for the unknown she'd been fighting off the past few months. Seeing him this way raised her lust level up a few more degrees. Now she understood why some women followed athletes around—it was out of lust.

Pure lust for the perfectly formed male body.

"Time to shower and go." He tossed the belt at her.

* * * *

Shadoe stormed into the locker room, shoved the door, and knocked some unsuspecting guy into the wall. He peeled off his clothing and left the items in a heap on the floor of the locker. The sound of cold steel hitting the wall echoed through the room, and he stalked away nude to the showers. Turning on the cold water full blast, he let out a blood-curdling howl that would've stopped a charging bull from going near him.

"Damn woman."

He twisted the other metal knob, and hot mixed in with the cold to melt the building frustration.

He could never quite figure out why he always had to test a woman. He'd issued a challenge of some sort in search of a blazing fire that would eternally ignite his hot passions.

He searched for the impossible. He'd have better luck looking for the pot of gold at the rainbow's end than searching for the perfect match to his passion.

"I thought all this bullshit would be easy. I thought she would be different." He scrubbed harder on his body at the discontentment, not caring who did or didn't hear him.

You idiot, she is different. Remember, that's what first attracted you to her? She's not interested in anything more than her career.

"I'm just a means to the end at this point, and there's no one but myself to blame for it."

If the meeting with Scott hadn't taken so long, he would've caught his original flight out of Madison. Instead, he had to go through each portfolio and handpick who he wanted to write the damn article. He'd never bargained for a woman like Khristen when he made his final decision before running out to catch the next flight to L.A.

Something had clicked in his mind when Khristen had reclaimed her seat on that flight. He'd counted his blessings that he'd left his shades on, certain his eyes would've given him away. The second he'd seen her soft, voluptuous curves, his senses had sent a signal rushing through his body. He'd been sure the windows of his soul were reflecting that sudden surge of desire.

This one hadn't backed down from him, at all. His size and demeanor hadn't even caused her to flinch for a second. He recalled damning his sometimes uncontrollable, arrogant manner for his smart-aleck responses. The look in those cool brown eyes had challenged him, and he'd found it hard to resist trying to unnerve the determination and confidence shining from their depths.

"If it hadn't been for her luggage tag, I never would've known who she was. At that point, it didn't really seem to matter. We were already on a collision course," he remembered, wondering whether things would ever be different between them.

Then, out of the blue, there she was, walking

along the beach of his hotel, her seductive curves outlined in a dress as the soft morning light filtered through it. How alluring she'd looked with the wind blowing through her hair and molding the white garment to her form. The new morning sun revealed a soft nakedness under the flowing material as she stopped to pick something up off the shore.

"Scott never mentioned she was beautiful, or where she was going on vacation—some minor details that may have prevented this entire situation. Some newspaper man he is, leaving out the key elements."

For one fleeting moment, Shadoe had considered approaching her, apologizing for his bad behavior. But, remembering the incident on the plane, he had thought better of it.

"Some plan, Donovan. You almost blew it, if you haven't already."

He rinsed the lather from his hair and then towel dried his body with vigor.

She'd looked so beautiful that afternoon as she brilliantly countered his challenge. She'd passed his little test; women usually lusted after him. Not only for his body, which was firm and solid without being muscle-bound, but also because of his career.

Obviously, Khristen wasn't impressed.

More than likely, once this assignment was done, she'd quit the magazine and vanish.

Then what would he do? Follow her around like a lost puppy?

Not on my worst day will I allow that to happen!

Still, Shadoe imagined the feel of Khristen in

his arms as he sat on the end of a bench. He felt her warmth all the way through his skin-tight jeans. The smell of her jasmine perfume filled his senses. He envisioned the softness of her hair barely touching his chest. Pulling on a pair of roper boots, Shadoe left the locker room carefully fastening the last button of his cotton shirt.

* * * *

Khristen picked up the wide leather belt still moist from his sweating body. The smell of damp leather and Shadoe's physique stirred deep-seated emotions—silly emotions that had first taken root in Hawaii, the land of romance, romantic notions that very well may have led her further down Heartbreak Pass.

Notions that have been nipped in the bud.

Maybe she had overreacted. Maybe she'd been just a touch unprofessional. Maybe her notions were both wrong. Maybe.

I guess I deserve this after slapping him last night. That doesn't change the fact that he lied to me. Or at least hid the truth. What's the difference? The point is he deceived me, right? Right.

She stroked the belt absentmindedly, like a mother stroking a sleeping child's hair, forgiveness already warming her heart.

She'd never realized what type of conditioning it took to be a professional in this world of body slams and elbow smashes. She'd seen it with each lift of the weights—that look of raw determination and dedication for something one loves more than life itself.

Maybe she'd judged the sport too harshly, after

all. Then again, maybe not. This wasn't a game of golf; it was purely physical and pushed the competitors well past their limitations.

It all seems so brutish, even violent at times. Heads being busted open from hits on an uncovered turnbuckle, or limbs nearly broken after being twisted into an unnatural position.

Everything had been so perfect up until the past twenty-four hours.

Why did he hide the truth from me? Is he ashamed of being a wrestler?

No, not after what I just witnessed. A person doesn't go through the kind of grueling workout he just did for a career he doesn't enjoy, and he doesn't defend every negative word implied about pro wrestling. His love runs deep, too deep for a mere mortal woman to combat.

The animal look in his eye last night after entering the ring had frightened her. It was as if some evil demon suddenly possessed his body the second he stepped through the ropes. Then it disappeared just as quickly once the bell rang out his victory. He was a man—no, an animal—poised for survival in what he considered to be the fight for life.

In a way, that's just what it was—a battle for his placement in the rankings. To be a money-winner, to keep the fans in a frenzy until he had his opponent's shoulders down on the mat for the three-count. It was what scared her most.

No wonder the youth of today were more aggressive than in generations before. If a person really thought about it, football and soccer could be just as violent, only in a different manner.

She knew it was going to be difficult to understand, and being objective in her reporting would be even tougher. A greater challenge yet would be the task of keeping her heart and desires in check.

She now knew both sides of that challenge and knew the challenge by one name. A name she'd grown too fond of.

Shadoe.

She shook her head, vaguely aware that someone had spoken. "What?"

Her heart quickened when the strap was pulled out of her grasp. She took deep breaths to relax her tense body and to regain some level of self-control.

"Time to go, sweetheart," Shadoe said.

His eyes clouded over before he left her shaking in her sandals. The look had been a controlled, cold one, not like any Shadoe had ever given her before. Flame was in control right now; she recognized that look from the ring. She was to be his next victim, the next in line to learn a lesson as only Flame could teach it. A shudder went through her bones when she followed him out to the car, despite the ninety-degree weather.

CHAPTER 9

"Wilder suggested I take you into a training camp," Shadoe said. "At first I was against it, but that was then, and this is now. You need a complete understanding of things, Khristen. Since I'm to be your target person, it looks like we're stuck with each other."

"Great. That will give my readers more insight on this game you play."

"Game? You think this is nothing but a game? This is exactly what I mean! Man, are you deluded. Haven't you learned anything these past few weeks? Sure, we know how to take the falls and how to pull the punches, but let me give you a little something to chew on and digest regarding the subject. We're dealing with a lot of different personalities and levels of tempers.

"These personalities have clashed on more than one occasion outside the ring, as well. We're professionals but human. We have our faults, including myself." Shadoe pulled into traffic, only half-paying attention to the road, his mind focused on how he could get her to understand. He wasn't about to give up on her. One way or another, she'd have to come to understand—and maybe appreciate—his world.

"Give me a break. This is just a game you play. A legal excuse to beat up on some guy you outweigh by fifty pounds or more," she said.

The click of her seat belt clanked at the same moment Shadoe stepped on the gas in frustration. Tires squealing, the car surged into an opening in the morning traffic.

"Is that so?" Shadoe swept his hair off his face to reveal more than one series of scars. "I suppose these are self-inflicted because I just love to have the blood run down my face," he said. "Warm, sticky blood blinding me from being able to counter my opponent's moves. Making me weak from its loss. Oh, yeah, the feel of a suture needle is the biggest high I could ever experience. I thought you knew me better by now."

"Depends on who I'm with—Shadoe or Flame. I thought I knew Shadoe, but evidently, I was proven wrong when the truth about his profession came out. A lack of trust in me only proved that point even more. Flame, on the other hand, is a whole new being; one I'm not sure is even human," she said. "Or if I even like the character."

"Trust is the whole issue here, isn't it? Your hackles are up because I kept this hidden from you. Now I see the light. I have to tell you every move I make in order to keep peace. Well, here's a news flash, honey. The only people I need to answer to about my actions are my family. And unless you're some long lost sister my parents have kept hidden away in a remote mountain convent, you just don't fit the bill." He jammed the accelerator and wove in and out of traffic like a NASCAR driver. Not once did he look for oncoming cars. He was burning mad.

"Thank God I'm not a sister of yours, and if I was, I'd make sure to stay lost for an eternity knowing I was related to someone of your caliber," she remarked.

"And what's wrong with my caliber? I'm not some fly-by-night, bar-stool-sittin', beer-drinking slob," he said.

She screamed as a blast from a horn rocketed her back to reality. "That may be the first bit of truth I've heard come out of your mouth for some time. Will you watch where you're going?" She grabbed the dash with one hand and the car door with another. "You just about got us killed, you idiot."

"At least you're still thinking in terms of us, not just you."

"Don't let it go to your head. It was just a figure of speech."

"Now back to my caliber. Would you care to explain yourself further? After all, you were just concerned about my welfare, which can only leave me to believe you may just like my caliber." He afforded her a quick glance and smirk.

"Compassion, that's all it was. Compassion for another human being's life."

"Which human being—Shadoe or Flame?"

She blew out a breath. "You're so infuriating!"

"Just like our first meeting in Hawaii, right?"

"Only worse. This time, you're in control of our destination, and I have no idea where in the world we're going," she complained.

"Did I forget to tell you, or have you closed your mind to the fact that we're going into a training camp? Afraid that all your misconceived ideas will go by the wayside once you learn the truth, Khristen?"

* * * *

The disgust in his voice only fueled her anger. She'd heard over the past few weeks how many wrestlers cut themselves to boost the ratings. Whether or not they were asked to do so was another issue, altogether. Maybe he wasn't one of those guys, maybe he was; she didn't know, and she didn't really care.

She glared back at the smug smile and twinkle in his eye. She had forgotten. With all the bantering, she felt lucky to remember she was in a moving vehicle. That was, until his recklessness a moment before had almost made them hood ornaments.

What happened to the even-tempered man I've come to know? He's behaving like he first did in Hawaii. He acts as if he wants to pick a fight to see how high my temper could go, making me fall in love with him.

Wait a minute. Fall in love? Is that what happened? No way I'd ever fall for a guy like him.

She'd never know from one minute to the next who he was. Thank God they hadn't made love;

then it would be a lost cause. Once physical intimacy entered the picture, there'd be no turning back. There was still time to keep her defenses from crumbling.

Rebuilding the wall of defense was turning out to be a never-ending battle. Each time she laid a brick, he somehow knocked it down. At this rate, she'd be nothing more than jelly in his hands.

"Ooooooo!" she protested, stomping her foot on the floor mat.

"Was that an answer, or just your mating call?"

"Believe me, if it was my mating call to you, I'd make sure you could tell."

"Really." He wiggled his eyebrows at her in the most infuriating way.

"I'd have to swing from a vine, jump into a swamp, wrestle an alligator, and come out looking like I'd just stepped out of the latest girlie magazine," she said.

"And all for the sake of mating with me. Somehow, I'm glad I've missed it." The boyish grin was back on his face, and that trademark twinkle lit up his eyes.

He was a quick-change artist, all right. Yet, it really didn't alarm her as much as she wanted him to believe. Not as much as she wanted her heart to believe.

Now, that's my Shadoe. It's been so long since he smiled like that, I thought for sure he was lost for good.

She watched him, trying to figure out what he was thinking. She really did like him. And, yes, it had become more than that. She looked forward to his "surprise" visits. Maybe there was more to this than he'd been willing to share. Maybe, just maybe, he didn't love his career as much as he professed to.

Maybe he'd talk more openly to her if she'd tried a little honey instead of vinegar, give away a few secrets he kept so dear to his heart and soul.

Hey, a girl can try, can't she?

"Shadoe, what is it about your career that puts you on the defensive? You're so untrusting about it, yet I sense a need to trust someone."

Okay, let the sugar turn to syrup and run all over his defenses.

"Not just someone, Khristen." His voice was soft and wistful, like a boy longing for the BB gun his mother won't let him have.

Now, that's a small breakthrough, let's see how far he opens the door.

"Why not let me help you, then? Is it because of this sort of love-hate thing we've got going?"

"Love has nothing to do with it! Why is it whenever our names are intertwined in one way or another, someone mentions love? You'd think I wouldn't know if and when I was in love with a woman," he protested.

"Who's been saying that?"

"And, if I was in love with a woman, what makes him think it would even remotely be with you? For Pete's sake, all we do is bicker with each other these days. I'm not so sure we're even friends anymore, let alone in love."

"He? Who is he? Shadoe! Who is he?" she repeated.

What the heck is he talking about? I never

mentioned anything about us being in love.

"Huh?"

"Who's been saying all this stuff to you?"

"Just some guy. A new employee of mine, who may just find his ass out in the streets next time I need to touch base."

"Do you always talk about the people who work for you like that?"

Tread lightly; he's opened a new door for you to push on.

"Depends on whether or not they try to delve into my personal life. And this guy has enough guts to say what's really on his mind. Mmmmm, not such a bad quality, he just needs to know what he can and can't stick his nose into," he said.

"You own a business and are a professional wrestler?"

"Yes." That one word, simple as it was, echoed loudly in the car.

Khristen felt a door slam shut; silence abruptly filled the car. Just the mention of the word love really set him off. He reacted to it like it was the plague. So maybe this explained his actions lately, if someone was hassling him outside the ring. Her mind ran quickly over the information like a ticker tape at the bottom of the television.

Business owner? What kind of business could he possibly own where an employee would give him what for? Not many would stick their noses into the boss's life. This one he trusted, but why?

"Well, here we are."

He pulled the rented vehicle into a vast parking lot.

"The airport? I thought we were going to a training camp."

"We are, but not just yet. Wilder will make an appointment at the training facility, and there are a few matches already scheduled to work around. One of them being the championship."

"Championship," she asked.

"For the belt. I've got a match coming up in Hawaii against Skywalker for the gold."

"But isn't he—"

"Dangerous?"

"No. Crazy?"

"In the ring, he is. I've got a lot of mental preparation to do before then. Staying on the right track is going to be tough right now," he said.

"You can do it."

"Hope so. Come on, we've got a little while before boarding. Have to visit the little girl's room?"

"Among other things," she answered, pulling her bag onto her shoulder.

* * * *

Khristen became mesmerized by Shadoe's muscle-defined physique as he strolled with confidence away from her at the pay phones. It was the kind of male walk that turned the head of every female he passed. Jealousy seeped through her bones, burning her heart.

Deep, uncontrollable desire moistened Khristen's panties with his every stride. The tip of her tongue slid over her lips. She ached to feel the heat of his body, to taste the salt on his skin. She felt sure the warmth would burn out of control if it were ever fanned by his touch. Was she losing sight of her feelings with such lustful yearnings? She hoped not as Shadoe slipped out of sight.

"Business, not pleasure," she reminded herself, taking a deep breath to calm her quaking nerves. She whimpered softly and ducked behind the nearest payphone, placing a call with trembling fingers.

"*Plain Talk.*"

"Ric Scott, please." She tried to control the smoldering passion burning inside.

"Ric, here."

"Hey, anything new?" Confronting Rick wasn't an easy task for her. She'd never before questioned anything the magazine did, but this time, she was directly affected by the changes. As she saw it, she had a right to whatever information he had.

"Khristen? What's wrong, you sound shaken by something."

"Yeah, something," she whispered, "or someone."

"What's wrong?"

"Nothing I can't handle."

"What's he done this time?" Ric asked.

"Who?"

"Come off it, Khristen. Donovan, who else? Ever since you got this assignment, he's the only person who's been able to unnerve you."

"Ric, I just need a friend to talk with." Nervously shifting her body weight, she continued. "You are right, though, he does seem to know what buttons to push and when. But then, I'm sure he's had a lot of practice."

"How is the assignment coming?"

"As well as can be expected. We'll be going into a training camp sometime soon after the next round of matches. Which, by the way, as luck has it, will take me right back to Hawaii," she said.

"Really, the land of romance? Maybe you'll fall in love this time."

"With who, some island boy?" She laughed. It felt good letting go of that pent-up sexual energy stored in her.

"Sure, why not? A nice, quiet home with seven or eight kids tugging on your skirt. Not such a bad thought when you consider all the advantages to it."

"Name them."

"Calmness in your life. Living in a tropical setting, you wouldn't have to put up with Mr. Donovan anymore, or for that matter, the magazine," he said.

"Sorry, Ric, dear. I just got out of boring, and I don't want to have to live that way again."

"So, traveling with a bunch of egomaniacs is okay, then."

"When you've described what life could be like otherwise, yes," she said.

Good ol' reliable Ric always knew how to bring a smile to her face. The vision he conjured up in her mind made her appreciate what she strived for a little bit more than she had before placing the call.

"Even where Shadoe is concerned? Even when he pushes those buttons of yours no one else has been able to find? Even then?" he asked, digging into her mind further.

"What are you getting at here, Ric?" She didn't like his line of questioning one bit.

"Oh, nothing. Just an observation on how bent out of shape you get about him sometimes; that's all."

"The man drives me nuts. I never know who I'm with—Shadoe or Flame. He can be sweet one minute and then get this wild animal look in his eye in a matter of seconds."

"I didn't know you'd ever been up close and personal with a wild animal before. Describe that look to me so I can better understand what you're seeing."

"What do you want here, blink by blink?"

"No, just tell me what you see in his face when that look magically appears."

"You're a man, for Christ sake. You should know better than I what I mean. Let me put it in words you can understand. It makes me feel either like prey to be toyed with, or a piece of flesh to be devoured. It's the same look he has in the ring."

"Khristen, I think you've been out of the dating game too long. Going on my knowledge of male looks, I'd have to say the one you are personally getting is one of prey to be devoured sexually," he said.

"Not in your wildest dreams," she protested.

"And how, may I ask, do you know anything about wild dreams? Been having a few of your own lately?"

Khristen's face warmed at the sudden emergence of her nightly visits with Shadoe in a world he couldn't physically interrupt.

"That's what I thought," he said. "Khristen, I think you're head over heels in love with the man and can't handle it."

"Ohhhh!" Khristen slammed the phone back into its cradle.

* * * *

Shadoe glanced down the hall, looking for Khristen, before coming out of the men's restroom. He spotted her with her arms flying through the air. He could only guess with whom she was having a war of words, and he didn't like it one bit.

Carefully, he went to the phones on the other side of the men's room and chose one where he could easily watch her finish the call. He needed to put a call in to the magazine himself, and now would be the most logical time, while she remained occupied.

Tapping the screen of his cell phone, he placed a call to Ric Scott. He wanted his editor-in-chief to be aware of the situation that would take place somewhere between there and Maui. A potentially dangerous situation, to say the least. Dangerous to his heart.

"Put me through to Scott."

He didn't give the person on the other end a chance to respond after picking up the receiver. He had no time for office etiquette or politeness at this point.

"He's on another call. Would you like to leave a message, or—"

"I'll hold."

He waited and watched Khristen go through a serious of animated actions while still on her call. A smile crossed his face as she shoved the phone into her purse and then stormed into the ladies' room. He felt confident someone just got an earful of frustration on the other end of the defenseless instrument. That someone had to be Ric Scott.

"I'll put you through now," the voice on the other end informed him.

"Ric Scott here."

Ric's voice was edged with laughter.

"And what's so funny, Scott?" Shadoe knew the answer. He didn't need to be told it was Ric Scott who'd just received the tongue-lashing Khristen had been giving.

"Donovan, what a coincidence," Ric replied. "I knew your call couldn't be too far behind Khristen's. You two are certainly a pair, aren't you?"

"Your point?" Shadoe asked.

"Well, let's see here. Animalistic looks of something wild and free about to claim its mate." Ric answered in between his laughter before continuing. "I believe the point to be made is love. And you've both been pierced by Cupid's sharp little arrow," Ric stated point-blank.

"Love. You and that damn word! Is that all your vocabulary consists of? Or is anything over four letters long too complicated for you to sound out?"

"See, you both react the same way. As soon as you two admit it to each other, 'cause I'm sure the entire world can see it, things may get back to some sort of normalcy around here," Ric replied. "Then all you've got to do is work on the honesty part, which, in case you've forgotten, Khristen's very big on. Come clean, Donovan."

Shadoe groaned into the phone. When he got back to Wisconsin, he was going to remind Mr. Ric Scott just what his duties at the magazine were, and they didn't include "Matchmaker."

"It won't hurt too much. You may even decide to make it a lifelong habit," Ric said.

"Funny you should bring up the concept of honesty because that's exactly what the plan for today is." Shadoe kept a watchful eye on the bathrooms. The last thing he needed right now was Khristen sneaking up on him.

"A plan? You mean to tell me you actually have a plan? That's rich!"

"I've decided to tell Khristen about the magazine and my part in it. I thought you should be aware of it. I'm sure you'll be the first person she calls," Shadoe said.

She usually does. The thought left a sour taste in his mind.

One day, she'll stand on her own and not run to Scott every time things start to heat up between us.

"No doubt. And when is this game of 'Truth or Consequences' going to happen?"

Good. He's worried. He should be; he's just as much a part of this little white lie as I am.

"Somewhere in the air between here and Maui. I figure there'd be nowhere for her to run, and she'll have no choice but to listen to me," Shadoe said. He turned his back to the bathrooms as Khristen came out and headed toward him.

"Not only are you taking your own life into

your hands, but also the lives of every innocent passenger on that plane. Being gutless is not a fault you carry on your shoulders, that's for sure."

"Gotta go. We'll be boarding, and she's coming," Shadoe said, his words flowing fast and hard.

"Thanks for the warning. I'll watch the news for a plane crash over the Pacific."

CHAPTER 10

"You're just in time. They've made the final boarding call for our flight." Shadoe took Khristen by the elbow, leading her down the terminal hall.

"Shadoe, for Pete's sake. I can walk there on my own. I'm not some little old lady to be led around." She pulled her arm out of his grasp.

"What's bugging you now?" He blessed her with that charming boyish grin of his. "No soap in the dispenser? Couldn't get into the stall fast enough? Or bad phone vibes?"

The tone of his voice sounded anything but charming. It betrayed his forced playful expression. Sarcastic and annoyed fit the mood he portrayed more than anything else.

What in his feeble little mind is he going to jump on me for now? It's not like I can just pull the zipper down and whip it out, for crying out loud.

She swept past him, knowing full well he was right behind her. Her senses alive and alert, she could feel him drawing nearer.

He had something on his mind, and she wasn't about to be the wall taking the force of his verbal blows. She'd been down that route before and possessed no desire to do so again, no matter how attracted to him she'd become. She wouldn't allow the passion he ignited in her heart and soul to overrule the faint warning bells echoing in her mind.

"I don't think what I do or who I talk to is really any of your business," she said. She wanted to be as obnoxious as he was. She wanted him to know how it felt to be talked to as if his presence was a bother, an inconvenience to those around him. She wanted him to feel her desire to put him in his place.

"I didn't think you'd ever surface from the bathroom again. I don't care to know about what topic of conversation goes on in there, either."

He sounded as if he hadn't heard a word she'd said. His tone was what she believed to be feigned concern for her well being. His mouth poised like a pouting little boy, it took all she had to turn away and hide the smile threatening to break across her face. If he was faking, he did an excellent job of acting the hurt little boy.

"A girl's got to do what a girl's got to do," she remarked.

Doesn't he ever come out of the acting long enough to be real anymore?

She wanted so badly to believe he truly worried about her, knowing full well he didn't. She shook her head, even though she knew he did have business to attend to. If he missed this flight to Maui, it wouldn't be the wisest move.

His livelihood and the championship belt would be on the line in less than forty-eight hours. She'd come to understand little-by-little why a heavy, gold-plated belt took precedence over anything and anyone in his life. It still amazed her, but she understood...a little.

She had a championship of her own to fight...hanging on to her heart and keeping her good sense about her. Still, there wasn't a reason important enough for her to stand there and take his best shot at word slinging—not without a good fight on her part.

"This just isn't the time for last-minute face adjustments, or whatever else it is women do in the bathroom. We've got a plane to catch."

He once again reached out to grasp her elbow.

"Then let's go and get seated," she snapped.

So, it was missing the plane and not what may have been taking me so long, by his standards, upsetting his precious order of life. No surprise there.

She sighed in defeat, disappointment moving in one giant wave through her soul. She moved forward to avoid his grasp, not wanting to give him the chance, or pleasure, of escorting her to the plane.

Why the sudden change in attitude? One minute, he'd been teasing and smiling, even the twinkle was back in his eye, and now just the opposite. Oh, the controlling games men played. She was already sick of the whole thing.

Suddenly she realized the change had occurred after the phone call moments ago. He hadn't looked all that thrilled when she came out of the bathroom. When their gazes met briefly, there'd been a relieved, yet serious look crossing his before he turned his back to her. The irritated look on his face had to be caused by that call. After the past forty-eight hours, she couldn't believe it being anything else. Her heart wouldn't let her.

She considered the possibility that their relationship, one starting as friendship, had turned into a convenience for him and his profession. Her promotion certainly worked to his benefit, maybe even more than to hers. Or was it her own insecurities and relationship misgivings making her feel this way?

What would he have to gain by using her? He hadn't put her in the current position of traveling with him. They'd been victims of fate, nothing more, a writing in the stars neither one of them had any control over.

Right? Right.

Shadoe's essence was always all over her, covering her soul and heart like a warm blanket. She thought it funny how comfortable and natural it felt to be at his side. They seemed to fit so well, maybe too well. That was where the problem had to be—the fit was too good.

She glanced at him as the stewardess took her boarding pass, realizing there was nothing she wouldn't…couldn't forgive him for...in time. How could she not be in love with him?

* * * *

Walking through the curtains into first class, Shadoe placed his hand on the small of Khristen's back and felt surging electricity each time her hip swayed. An ache grew deep in his loins, and heat rose to the top of his head. Man, she had a way of making him forget his common sense and the reason for her being there in the first place. The way her skin warmed his with just a touch was enough to ignite a forest fire.

No escape route. Relief blew through him in the wake of the thought. *Play it safe, my man. Wait until we're airborne.*

"I see you've taken my seat, Ms. Roberts," he said.

He looked away from her star-filled eyes with a deep, silent sigh and allowed his thoughts to return to business. *I don't know which is going to be worse—trying to keep the gold around my waist, or trying to get hold of something more precious.*

"Your seat?" she asked, a smile twitching at the corners of her mouth. "I didn't realize it was yours. If my mind serves me right, Mr. Donovan, the situation was just the opposite several months ago."

"Several months ago, I didn't know whom I was dealing with."

He was desperate to keep the seriousness in his voice, not wanting to give away any of his feelings. He couldn't afford for her to know that a part of him would die without her near him. She'd become the solid ground he needed in which to take root.

"You mean to tell me it makes a difference?" she asked.

The landscape passed by the window as the

plane taxied onto the runway. He wished he could just hop out the window and land safely on his feet. He likened it to his feelings toward the situation with her. *Land on my feet and keep my head high. Heart in one piece. Soul full of her light.*

"Sure it does. It's like getting to know your opponent before a match. If the opponent is worth your time and energy, you study tapes, learn how to counter his moves, and then move in for the kill."

His pulse raced faster along with the speed of the plane before it left the ground. She pulled the window cover down and then took a hunting magazine from behind the seat facing her.

"Tell you what, why don't you think about how you're going to explain that little lesson of total destruction while reading this," she said.

Splat! She slapped him in the chest with the magazine, a smile curling at the corner of her full mouth. One challenge after another—that was what their friendship had turned out to be.

"And why don't you just go off in some little dream world safe from all the monsters this universe has bestowed upon you. I'll tell you when we've arrived in your make-believe world."

Khristen glared daggers at him.

He opened the magazine and ignored her maddening heavy breathing. Right then, he couldn't afford to be soft and willing. She didn't deserve the hardened attitude he'd given her just because he couldn't guarantee his own actions. He'd been unfair, but he'd maintained the front and kept Khristen off guard. Their future depended on it.

Their future. How many times over the past

forty-eight hours had that concept grown to become more? More times than he'd thought possible. More than the desire he once had to be the best in the ring at all costs.

Funny how all it takes is the right woman in the right place in time to change a man.

He never would've guessed buying a small-time magazine would lead him to something more valuable, or how looking for a fresh, unheard voice would take him down a path he'd fought so hard to stay away from over the years. The game changed, yet the rules stayed the same. *No holds barred and no disqualification.*

* * * *

Khristen came up through the shadows of sleep, sliding a hand across her ear as a light draft passed over the side of her face. Where was a draft in the plane coming from? She opened her eyes and caught Shadoe as he leaned over to lightly blow through hair that had fallen over her ear.

"Wake up, sleepy head." The whispered words came dangerously close to her ear, igniting her sexual need for him.

"I hope you have a good reason for waking me," Khristen replied. *Let alone come as close as a lover would.* She put her seat in its upright position and stretched out her cramped muscles.

"Of course."

Shadoe reached across her breasts to open the window covering. If he turned a little more inward, she'd be in his embrace, trembling as she was now. Hell, they'd have the opportunity to be members of the mile-high club if he didn't back off and soon!

"We'll be landing shortly, and we need to talk," he said.

"We talk all the time, Shadoe," she replied quietly, even though she could see that this was important. All the evidence was there—tone of voice, brows furrowed, the twinkle in his eye replaced by an apprehensive look. Important didn't even touch it. Serious, most likely. Shadoe never looked apprehensive about anything.

"What's on your mind?" She waited patiently for him to start, knowing not to push.

He let out a deep, heavy sigh and looked around to be sure of their privacy.

"Well, first of all, I was totally wrong in not telling you, up front, who I was and what I did for a living. For that, I'm sorry. I can only hope that when you hear the whole story, you'll understand my reasons and position."

"Duly noted."

He took her hand in his, sending hot shivers of desire shooting up her spine.

"You have to understand something Khristen," he said. He played with her fingers one by one. "Our meeting wasn't a planned one. I'd missed my actual flight due to a business transaction taking a little longer than I'd anticipated."

"So what you're saying is that destiny, fate, brought us together that day?" *Boy, what line of bull is he spewing now? Mushy crap some barfly might swallow. Not me, though.*

"In some ways, yes. But in a lot of ways, no." Shadoe swallowed hard, the rise and fall of his Adam's apple calling out an invitation for a flick of her tongue, and then closed his eyes.

"I'd been finishing up the final arrangements with the company manager about the employees in the office. I was looking for someone with the desire, drive, and ethical mind to perform a certain duty. Someone who'd never been given the opportunity but craved it in their soul."

She was confused by the seriousness of not only his voice but also the look in his eye. Whatever he had to tell her scared him to death, and for whatever reason, he felt he had to confide in her.

She put her hand over his in hopes it would encourage him to continue.

"I bought a small press magazine and needed someone to write an article for me," he said.

Khristen pulled her hand from his as the light bulb went on in her mind. She felt as if her breath was suddenly yanked from her body, and her world was in a tailspin.

"*Plain Talk*? You're the mysterious new owner?"

She saw nothing, yet everything. Her dream crashed into the depths of a nightmare.

"Yes. But I didn't know the writer I'd assigned to do the piece was you. I knew your name but didn't know it was you until we struggled over your bag on the plane."

"You've known all this time and not once did you find it necessary to tell me?"

She leaned further away from him, away from the deceit and lies. *That is all this man seems to know. Truth isn't a part of his life. Trust is something locked behind an iron door.*

"I didn't know how to tell you..."

"You didn't know... How about when I got the call from Ric... My God, Ric's known all along."

"Yes, I ordered him to keep it under wraps." He touched her shoulder.

"Don't touch me! Don't you ever touch me again," she cried. She got out of her seat, pushed past him, and headed down the aisle.

Trapped. She had to run but had nowhere to go, nowhere to escape from this nightmare.

How could I have ever thought I had any feelings for that man? He knows only how to be deceitful and use people for his own gain. He's shattered every dream I ever had. He's broken my heart beyond, and this time, he can't fix it.

I have to get off the plane and away from Shadoe…but where can I go? We're thousands of feet above the earth.

It would be another half an hour before they'd land in Los Angeles. She staggered down the aisle to the only sanctuary she could think of—the bathroom. She thanked the gods it was unoccupied and stepped inside. Relief swept through her like a tornado when the door clicked shut; she all but sank to her knees. Tears streamed down her cheeks from the pain stabbing her heart to death.

She pushed herself from the only barrier between her and Shadoe. She couldn't believe this was happening. She brushed unshed tears from her eyes and then took a deep breath to steady herself. "Do I have a big 'L' or the word 'stupid' painted on my forehead?"

The reflection in the mirror fought to keep

more of the tears from slipping over already dampened cheeks.

"Must be a sign only men like Shadoe can detect."

Khristen grabbed a tissue and blew her nose. The anger replaced the hurt aching in her.

"Ladies and gentlemen, please return to your seats. We'll be landing at LAX in ten minutes. The temperature is a balmy..."

There are only minutes left. Then what? She'd have no alternative but to continue on to Maui... *But I'll be damned if I do it on the same flight as that so-called man!*

She had to get off in Los Angeles, catch the next flight, and somehow get to the bottom of this entire nightmare.

She left the closet-sized bathroom, slipped into the first vacant seat, and then snapped the safety belt into place with renewed purpose.

How'd I manage to be fooled by all this?

The answer came easy enough—two men hitting her heart at the same time with lies plentiful enough to confuse a priest.

Once again, she'd let her heart override her common sense. She'd let Shadoe open that bolted door. She'd practically handed him the key to unlock it.

Khristen sank deeper into her seat as the plane landed on the runway. With the slight bump, she realized she was in too deep this time, deeper than any hole a bomb could have made. Her heart had exploded, and she didn't know if she'd ever be able to piece it back together again. Khristen left her seat and prepared to depart with the rest of the passengers flying coach.

CHAPTER 11

Shadoe looked in desperation for the one woman who meant more to him than any belt made of gold and diamonds. His spirit slipped in a downward spiral into a bottomless darkness. Should he get up and look for her, try to say the things he didn't get a chance to before she'd cringed at his touch and left him with tears pooling in her eyes?

No, chances are I'll stick my size thirteens into my big mouth all over again.

Where could she have gone?

They hadn't landed in Los Angeles, and yet, there was no sign of her. Once she'd gotten through coach, he'd lost sight of her.

God, help me. If I could take back my words, I would in a heartbeat. I'd find a way to explain myself better, so the hurt on her face wasn't there... But really, what did I expect after deceiving her all this time? That she'd wrap her arms around me, say she understood the lies, and then forgive me for the past few months? Not in this lifetime, nor any other, for that matter.

Of that, he was sure.

"Damn." He settled back into his seat. "You lost big time, Donovan."

As he saw it, there was only one thing to do, one person he could turn to for help. Ric Scott, the man who knew Khristen better than she knew herself. He took out his cell phone and tapped in the number for Scott's office. For once in his life, Shadoe had lost control of a situation and found himself turning to someone for guidance. He felt damned for all time.

"Excuse me, Mr. Donovan, but you'll have to finish that call after we land. It'll interfere with communication between the pilot and the air traffic control tower."

"How long before we land?" he asked the flight attendant.

Shadoe felt time slip effortlessly out of his hands as he disconnected the phone call. Control was no longer his. He'd become a servant to the situation, not the master.

"The seat belt sign has come on, so it should be about fifteen minutes before you can make your call."

"Fifteen... Have you seen my companion, Ms. Roberts?" His voice sounded pleading even to his ears. *When did I become so desperate to make amends with a woman?*

He knew all too well when. On a plane just like the one he was in, heading in the same direction, to the same airport.

"Oh, yes. She went into the restroom at the other end of the plane. Would you like me to ask her to return to her seat?"

"No. I'm sure she'll be back before we land," he said, praying he was right. The departure door was in front of him, and he had a sick feeling Khristen was going to walk right through it and straight out of his life.

If she did disappear, he'd have no choice but to call Scott, to warn him of the entire situation, if nothing else. Once they landed, he'd make damn sure his call was put through without hesitation or delay.

"...LAX in ten minutes. The temperature is...."

She's going to leave, there's no doubt about it now.

Shadoe's heart hit rock bottom as the plane's landing gear connected with the runway pavement. His hopes and dreams faded away with the slow movement of the plane as it taxied to its gate. The greatest love in his lifetime would vanish as soon as the door opened.

No!

He swore an oath under his breath, slamming his fist down. "Not like this. Not without her knowing how I feel about her. Not without the full story is she going to walk out of my life. No way. No how."

The plane came to a complete stop, and Shadoe tapped on his phone again. He didn't care who told him to terminate the call this time. He needed to talk to Scott, possibly the only lifeline he had, and he wasn't about to let it slip away.

Shadoe waited for Scott to answer the private line as Khristen left with the Los Angeles passengers. The phone rang only a few times, but it felt more like eternity before Scott answered.

The voice of Shadoe's savior came over the line. "Hello."

"Scott, it's Donovan." Shadoe could only hope he sounded more in control than he really was. "I need your help."

Silence as black as night followed, as if they had been cut off.

"Where is she, Shadoe?" Scott's voice was quiet. Too quiet.

"I don't know," he answered. "What did you call me?"

Shadoe. He called me by my first name. Lord, am I in for it now. I can't blame the guy; he knows her better than I do. I should have listened, but once again, I want to be in charge of everything.

"Shadoe, do you know where Khristen is?" Scott asked again, his voice eerily calm and controlled.

"No. We've landed in LA. She didn't come back to her seat after she walked away. She may have gotten off the plane. At least, I don't see her. Yes, I'm sure she got off." His stomach churned, and a sick feeling crept its way into his heart.

"You told her, then? The whole thing?"

"As much as I could before she got up and never came back." Shadoe wished he could get back the past two hours of his life.

"How much, Donovan? How much does she know?"

Ah, that was more like it. Back to the routine of using last names. It was the start of strength Shadoe needed.

"Watch your tone, Scott," he warned, knowing full well it fell on deaf ears. "She knows I own the magazine, that I didn't initially know who she was. That's as far as I got before she took off. I didn't get a chance to get into any details." Shadoe said.

"Shit!"

"She put together that you've known all along and didn't tell her. I assured her you were under orders from me not to say anything to her." Shadoe tried to explain.

"You know she's going to call, don't you?"

"I'm counting on it, Scott." Shadoe felt his confidence sink further. "The way I figure it, she'll make the call as soon as she's got her head together."

"Maybe sooner than that, Donovan. If I know Khristen, she'll cool down after she blows my head off; then realize she's still got a job to do. You wanted integrity and ethical. Like I've said in the past, you've got it in her."

Shadoe vanquished the shakiness out of his voice. "I'm going on to Maui, then."

"I'll call if I hear anything."

"You damn well better, Scott. Your job depends on it."

Shadoe cut off the call as the Maui-bound passengers took their seats. As confident as he tried to sound with Scott, he wasn't sure whether Khristen would see him again once he found her. How could he blame her? He damn well knew how it looked. This time, she was wrong. He'd prove it to her, one way or another.

Shadoe snapped his seat belt into place, barely hearing the pilot or the feeling the lift of the plane as it left the ground. All he had on his mind were the two biggest battles in his life meeting head-on. He wondered whether he was strong enough to fight both and still come out victorious in the one that mattered most.

* * * *

Khristen watched from the window as the man she loved and despised was carried into the sky far away from her. She wanted to confront him, now that the anger had settled down some, but she'd been too late to re-board the plane. Too late to come to her decision. Too late to tell Shadoe to find another writer. Just, too late.

She dabbed at the tears on her cheek and turned from the sight to set out looking for the nearest private area. Now, unless she could talk to Ric and convince him she was through, she'd have to go on to Maui. She'd have to finish the assignment and then quit. That was exactly what she'd do—have a good, long talk with Ric, complete the story, and then walk away with what was left of her heart.

How am I ever going to get to Maui now?

Everything she had with her was on the plane now thousands of miles in the air—including her ticket tucked safely inside her carryon bag in the overhead compartment.

She stopped one of the boarding gate attendants as a sense of panic enveloped her soul. "Excuse me."

"Yes, may I help you?"

"I hope so. I missed my flight...that flight," Khristen said.

Khristen played the situation on the fly. She turned and pointed out the window to the small figure of the plane that carried her heart hundreds of miles away. Another tear slipped down her cheek as she turned back to the woman.

"Actually, I was on the plane when my...my husband and I..." Khristen said. "We were on our honeymoon when we..."

She didn't bother to wipe the moisture from her eyes.

Husband? Did I just say husband? What am I thinking?

She looked away from the woman waiting for her to finish the trumped up explanation.

"Had an argument?"

Khristen felt the light touch of a hand on her shoulder. It felt like a touch of understanding and sympathy.

Khristen continued walking with her companion down the hall, toward the ticket counter. "More like a misunderstanding. I thought—"

"You'd be able to get off the plane, cool down, then re-board before the flight continued on?"

"Yes."

Khristen remained sheepish and prayed her little performance was convincing. She watched for any change of expression at the realization of the lie. It really wasn't a lie, after all. Okay, the husband part was but not the rest.

"Come on, let's see if we can get you on the

next flight. But don't get your hopes up too high; we'll need some kind of identification."

"Yes and no. My ticket is in my bag, and that's in the overhead compartment on its way to Maui," she said, pulling out her driver's license, which she'd tucked into her front pocket after boarding. "But will this help any?"

She handed the state-issued driver's license over to the attendant, praying it was enough to get her on the next flight.

"I'll see what I can do. No promises, though." She smiled weakly and then walked over to the gate's desk.

Emptiness squeezed Khristen's heart The man she had spent so much time with was now somewhere over the Pacific Ocean thousands of miles away from her. Then there was a man who was more like a brother than a friend most likely sitting behind a desk of deceit, feeling heaven knew what. The two of them, different yet so much alike, had taken her heart and ripped it apart.

Shadoe had gained her trust and captured her soul to use for his own selfish reasons. It no longer mattered he hadn't known who she was at first. What did matter was the fact he didn't have enough respect for her to tell her about the magazine. It wasn't like he'd never had the chance; they were together all the time.

And Ric, what was she going to do about him? Could he have laid his career on the line for her? If not, what were his reasons? She could just about imagine.

Something to do with love, no doubt.

That always seemed to be his answer to everything these days concerning herself and Shadoe.

"Ms. Roberts?"

"Yes," Khristen replied, her stomach churning in anticipation of bad news.

"If you hurry, we can get you back to the boarding gate. A plane leaves in fifteen minutes for Maui."

"Thank you."

Moisture pooled in her eyes once again. Without hesitation, she turned and jogged back down the path she'd just traveled—a path that would lead her to either total destruction or a lifetime of happiness. Either way, she'd deal with it as it came, this time. It was her choice, and she chose to go on to Maui. She'd complete her assignment from a distance without Shadoe knowing she was there. She wouldn't call in to the magazine until she was back on the mainland with a completed article. After that, she had no idea. She'd travel that road as it rose up to meet her.

* * * *

A shiver passed through his body as Shadoe shifted in his seat. His mouth felt bone-dry and his body clammy with perspiration. Not sure whether it was from fear or ecstasy, he let out a moan and rolled his head from side to side. He gripped the arms of his seat as his body jolted sideways.

"Mr. Donovan?"

He woke with a start at the sound of his name. Slowly, he focused in on the face bending towards him.

"I'm sorry to disturb you, but your phone has been ringing since we touched down."

"Hmm, thank you."

He stretched before righting his seat and then pulled the cell phone out from his jacket. He ran a hand through his hair, hoping against hope it was Khristen.

"Yeah."

It was all he could manage to say through the grogginess.

"Donovan, it's Scott."

Disappointment soared through him at the same time his heart fell through the bottom of his stomach.

"Have you heard anything?" Shadoe asked, looking out the window as the pavement slid under the plane going into the gate.

"Nothing. And it worries me."

Shadoe felt the same cold shiver of fear he detected in Ric Scott's voice. "Where is she?"

"That's what I'd like to know." Scott's concern edged his words. "This isn't like her at all. Just what in the hell have you done to her these past few months, Donovan?"

"Say what?" Anger mixed with a very scared feeling. Shadoe felt moisture beading on his lower lip. His heart thumped hard and fast against his ribs.

"You heard me. This isn't like Khristen at all to act so irresponsible and thoughtless."

"And you blame me for that? Just who in the hell do you think you are? Her father? She's a big girl. She isn't going to do anything stupid." He wasn't about to let Scott know just how scared he was about Khristen. Years in the ring had taught him how to perform. Now, he'd have to give a performance unlike any before.

"As if you care. All you've cared about is getting that damn story of yours and to hell with anyone else! The lime light..."

Shadoe remained silent as Scott continued to rant and rave. The man had every right to be concerned, and angry. For the life of him, he couldn't figure out where she'd gone either.

"...winning at all costs. You selfish..."

"I care about her, too, Scott."

Hell, he more than cared! He loved her. He'd give his life for hers if the need ever arose.

"No, you don't," Ric replied.

Shadoe looked out the window into the cloud-filled blue sky. "More than you know. More than you could ever imagine," Shadoe said quietly.

He hung up and questioned the powers that be. Did he know Khristen as well as he thought? Surely, she'd be in Maui before night's end.

CHAPTER 12

"Welcome back, Mr. Donovan. Your suite is ready, and we've followed your instructions."

"Thank you, Jennifer. Has Khristen Roberts checked in yet?" Shadoe dropped his bag, glancing, hopeful, around the lobby.

He knew it would be impossible since his flight arrived without her, but he wanted to know if there was any word at all from Khristen.

"Mmmm... No sir, not yet," Jennifer said after checking the guest list.

"Okay. When she does, ring my room right away, would you, please," he asked, making his way around the counter to his office.

"Yes, sir."

"Thanks again for your help, Jennifer." Shadoe glanced at the pile of papers on his desk, waiting for him to go through tomorrow. He walked out of his office with a heavy heart.

"Ah, Mr. Donovan?"

"Yes, what is it, Jennifer?"

"A message for you from Mr. Wilder."

He took the message, reading the words in silence:

Change in match. Cage is now no DQ; anything goes. Arrive early to work out details.

"Damn!" He grabbed his discarded bag and moved across the lobby to a private elevator. *What the hell? Has Wilder totally lost his mind?*

A last-minute change was the last thing he needed on his mind right now. Somehow, he'd have to bring Flame to the forefront. He'd have to find a way of forgetting the past few hours...and Khristen.

Once in his private suite, Shadoe dropped his bag at the door and took a long, deep breath. The match that night could end up being a career-ending one for either himself or Skywalker. So much had changed over the past few years. When he'd first entered the ring fifteen years before, a wrestler depended on his agility, strength, and stamina. Now the young lions coming into the arenas depended on slamming their opponents across tables and smashing heads with baseball bats and metal folding chairs. The business was more theatrical than anything else these days. Guys he'd come to know and love like family had either been crippled with serious injuries or died from stunts taken a step too far.

These days, ratings were far more important than the safety of those who performed in the ring. When had a person's life become so insignificant?

Five hours, and his life as he knew it could be over. It was already half-dead, as it was, without

Khristen by his side. That was a half of life completely unknown to Flame. The ring was what he knew and lived for night after night, city after city. Could he ever mesh the two? Would he be forced to give one up? After tonight, he'd know. He had to know where his life was headed and which one lived on...

Shadoe or Flame.

He could only afford to think about his wrestling career, the only life—and love—he'd ever really known and counted on all these years. Like a mistress of the night, the ring had always been there waiting for him to return, never asking where he'd been, or when he'd be back again. If this affair were destined to end, it would be on his terms and his terms only.

Shadoe stood over the weight lifting equipment sitting in front of the expansive glass patio doors looking out at the vast ocean and blue sky. The waves of the Pacific crashed along the beach. He shed his clothes and then turned from his naked reflection.

"Okay, let's do it."

His alter ego emerged from a restful sleep, and he readied for his match.

* * * *

Just before five o'clock, the shuttle pulled up in front of the hotel where, a few months before, her life had begun to change. Khristen stepped down and instructed the bellboy to leave her bags at the counter, and that she'd be checking in soon. She needed to think, needed time to build her defense against the memories the stone hotel structure held for her—against the man who, no doubt, was waiting to hear an explanation from her as to why she left him alone on the plane back in Los Angeles. She had to find the shut-off valve to the love flowing in her heart for him.

Slipping off her shoes, she padded through the cool green grass, up to the path leading to the patio garden. She smiled at the butterflies fluttering around the fragrant blooms and noticed something different about it this time—an entire section totally devoted to the orange Bird of Paradise, her favorite exotic flower.

"Ah, Shadoe." The memory of the bouquet he'd sent her flooded her mind. How could she not forgive him with the beautiful orange blooms staring her in the face?

She wiped away the tear sitting in the corner of her eye. They were the first and only flowers he'd ever sent her. On more than one occasion, he'd had them shipped in because the local florist didn't carry the expensive flower. Another unnoticed token she hadn't recognized and now wished she had.

She walked to the edge of the lawn and then stepped onto the patio, turning away from the reminder of his affection.

How can I shut down my feelings and walk away? Will I be strong enough to stay behind the scenes?

She wiped a tear from her cheek. Probably not, but she knew she'd have to try.

"Has Khristen checked in yet, Jennifer?"

"Shadoe," Khristen whispered through the

tightening of her throat. Heart tripling in rhythm and her blood pumping wildly through her veins, she quickly stepped into the early-evening shadows and hid around the corner to keep him from seeing her.

She chanced a peek around the corner of the open patio. Her heart skipped a beat seeing the way Shadoe stood slightly slumped at the desk. She'd never seen him appear to be so defeated before. It was a dangerous frame of mind with the big match tonight.

He sounded nervous about more than just her not checking in yet. Or was this another one of his acts? He wouldn't feign concern for her in front of a hotel employee; he'd wait and do it when they were face-to-face in hopes of breaking through her barriers.

She couldn't dismiss the fact he didn't act like a man about to go into battle. He acted like one about to be defeated.

"No sir, she hasn't."

"Damn! Where is she?" Irritation edged the concern of the words. "Jennifer, would you have someone bring my car?"

"Already waiting for you."

"Thanks." He turned and walked from the front counter, his head shaking slightly.

"Shadoe?" A young man asked from behind him.

His back straightened, and he swung his head around. "Yes?"

"Do you still want to know when Ms. Roberts arrives?"

"By messenger, immediately!" he demanded.

Khristen sank into a nearby chair, watching him walk out the front door. All the fight melted from her heart; there was only evidence of the love that had a grip tighter than any sleeper hold.

Should she run after him and proclaim her love before it was too late? No! Being strong and standing by her decision would be hard, but she had to protect herself from this path of destruction. She prayed Shadoe could do the same.

* * * *

Shadoe parked his white Jag and then walked through the back doors of the arena. Everything was in place—the filming crew, remote cameras, broadcast tables, ring, and the cage hanging high above the squared circle. In silence, he studied the square, five-sided metal box of chain link fence made to destroy the men battling inside it.

What the hell had he agreed to this time? The match had been signed months ago, and there'd been no mention of the match being "no disqualification" at that time. He had at the very least ten years on Skywalker, but a feeling deep in his gut told him it wouldn't be an advantage tonight.

The organization had become bloodthirsty of late. The more physical damage one could do to one's opponent, the better. Sky Walker was a prime example of that new mentality in the business—a mentality wrestlers like Shadoe found hard to abide by but did so because of the families they needed to provide for.

Violence.

The career he loved with heart and soul had

taken a turn into the darkest side of hell.

A feeling of doom haunted his heart. He knew where the power to change the road he walked on lay. He, alone, possessed such power. No one else could tell him what he needed to do or how to do it.

He started back toward the dressing room area to find Wilder but only took a few steps before the promoter sauntered up the aisle.

"Shadoe." Wilder stood just to the left of him.

"What's this all about?" Shadoe didn't take his eyes off him, noting the beads of sweat. "This has been signed for months as just an ordinary cage match."

"He issued the challenge, Shadoe. If you'd been paying attention, you'd have known it was coming. Let's take a walk; the doors will open any minute now."

Christ, a challenge I never knew about. Something's not right.

His world spun faster with each passing second. He'd seen this happen to those who'd walked the aisle before him. Now was it his turn? The organization may be telling him something he didn't want to hear. Bending over and kissing butt wasn't his way. The words weren't in his vocabulary.

"What's this all about, Tommy? And when was this challenge issued?" Shadoe asked.

Shadoe wanted to punch the wall. Instead, he pushed aside the curtained arena floor entrance and kept his actions in check. Wilder followed closely on Shadoe's heels like a dog sniffing out a bone.

"The other night in Rockford. After a match

with Thorp. He called you out for basically a street fight where anything and everything goes," Wilder said.

Shadoe stopped dead in his tracks and turned to face the man who was supposedly only the messenger. The hair on his arms prickled standing at attention. He fought to control the temper rising through his body.

Messenger, hell! Wilder is the instigator.

"Anything...meaning chairs, bats?"

Shadoe felt Flame begin to emerge as usual a few hours before a big match. His calmer, quieter side slipped away. "Whatever it takes to get my belt? Anything, that is, except pure physical ability."

"Pretty much," Wilder said. "You afraid of something? I can't believe the great Flame's hesitant to get into the ring tonight and defend that belt. You've gotten soft, Donovan."

Wilder's manner had an edge of shakiness Shadoe heard in his words. "The audience ate it up, loved it. The organization..."

"Is looking for bigger ratings." Shadoe finished the sentence for him, knowing full well what was being asked of him. "You go back to the organization and tell them they'll get what they asked for...and more."

Shadoe turned and headed for his private dressing room. He knew the routine, the pattern followed by those before him. Well, this time, they'd get what they demanded without really demanding it. Only he'd throw in a little twist of his own. Oh, yeah, just enough of a twist to make them take heed of his message...if they were really listening.

As he changed into his wrestling attire—trunks, pads and boots—he reflected on his life, his career. He'd worked hard to get to the top and even harder at staying there. No snot-nosed young punk was going to run roughshod over him without a fight.

He'd been luckier than most over the years, escaping with only minor injuries. Cuts. Bruised ribs. Sore muscles. So many others sustained major complications from pile drivers, spears, power slams, and jack knives. That was well before the chairs, bats, tables, guitars, and anything else not stationary became the norm in the ring. Up until this match, he'd been able to avoid those situations.

By God, I will continue that avoidance.

His plan for retirement didn't include collecting disability benefits.

This was to be a major pay-per-view event, and he wasn't about to let the opportunity slip by. He'd have to have an interview between matches, and the pre-approved script was about to change. A little bonus the federation hadn't bargained for.

He had too much to lose. His pride, reputation, and dignity were all at stake. The biggest thing, the most precious of all, was losing a possible future with a woman who'd stolen his heart thousands of miles above the ground.

He laced up his wrestling boots, thinking of the warriors who had fallen before him. He thought of Khristen and knew exactly what she'd come to mean to him. Oh, yeah, he knew exactly how tonight would end. Flame would go out in a blaze of glory.

* * * *

Khristen paced in front of the television, willing herself to leave the screen black and lifeless. She knew the matches were going on. She felt the unnerving sensation that Shadoe's was close at hand.

What am I afraid of? The fact I could care so deeply for a man who got his body beaten on a nightly basis? The fact I ran off without hearing his full explanation about the magazine? Or is it the love I feel every time I think of him?

Her finger pressed the button that brought the television to life. Staring into the camera, Flame had that unmistakable look in his eye. Rage already seethed through his veins. He was on fire, and the sound of his words brought that message clearly to the front of a battle that hadn't made it to the ring yet.

He grabbed the microphone from the interviewer. Silence filled the room. He studied the camera lens without so much as a twitch in his face. The message came through loud and clear. The challenge was being met.

"...Skywalker! Challenge me to the kind of fight that has no business going on in front of people."

Flame moved with determination closer to the camera, making his presence felt through the lens. Khristen found herself backing away from the rage in his eyes and the bloodlust in his words.

"No DQ. Street fight. Weapons of all kinds. What? You can't beat me on your physical ability, you need the chance to use chairs and bats and whatever else is handy..."

Her knees buckled out from under her, and she sank to the floor. Khristen heard what sounded like a gasp coming from somewhere in the room. Her heart pounded so fast and hard, she thought it would burst through her breast.

The match had been changed. He hadn't prepared for this type of match. He hadn't studied the tapes on Skywalker to find his faults and weaknesses. All because of her.

"...guess what buddy? I'm not playing the game like that. I'm going to beat you the same way I have everyone before you and walk out with the gold still around my waist."

Flame marched out of view of the camera, leaving the announcer mumbling and stammering.

"God, no!"

Khristen heard her cry of anguish. "He'll get killed. And it's my fault!"

She had to get to him, stop him from ending his career and totally destroying his body. She'd get down on her hands and knees and beg him not to fight tonight, if she had to.

Grabbing her bag on the way out the door, she didn't bother to wait for the elevator. Instead, she flew down the five flights of stairs and into the lobby. She ran over to the front desk short of breath and banged on the bell until someone came out.

"I need a car, now!" She was unaware of the tears slipping down her face.

"Right outside, Ms. Roberts. It's been waiting for you." Jennifer handed her a set of keys.

Khristen sprinted out the revolving doors into the night as if the hounds of hell were chasing her.

CHAPTER 13

Shadoe stood in the dark, waiting for his entrance music to begin, before pushing through the curtains and into Flame's world, a world where danger to his life and career lurked in every corner. A world where women like Khristen didn't exist, where someone soft, caring, and loving had no place. Not even outside those dark little corners.

"...beat you 'til you beg for mercy. Heed my warning, Flame! You'll be reduced to no more than..." The threat echoed through the arena.

Skywalker.

The name pushed all thoughts of Khristen from his mind as Flame emerged, and his music blasted from the arena speakers. One more breath and the transformation would be complete. The warrior would be fully awakened from the darkness of his mind within moments.

He took that last bit of air, feeling his real self melt into Flame. His body jolted back from the dark depths of his alter ego. He heard his birth name through the lifting veil.

"Mr. Donovan! Shadoe!"

Flame wasn't totally letting go of his mind and soul. He backed off only long enough for Shadoe to focus in on the young person who stood shaking in front of him.

"She's on her way here. She'll be here at any moment."

"Khristen." Her name barely a whisper, Flame retreated back to the darkness. Shadoe reemerged when the ring announcer's voice boomed over Flame's entrance music. It drew him from the image of her arrival and their reunion.

"...World Champion, Flame!"

He pushed through the curtains into the arena, pumping his fists into the air, only partially aware of the crowd, the ring, and the man determined to destroy him; a part of his mind wandered to Khristen being there. Khristen, the most precious person in his life, the only reason for his being.

Vaguely conscious of his journey down the aisle, Flame fought to bring himself into the game. He had to gain control, or he'd be mentally and physically destroyed. Suddenly, the odds bounced dangerously in Skywalker's favor.

He reached for the top rope and pulled himself into the ring, feeling eighty-percent sure Flame was in control. He'd settle for it; the other twenty percent would follow.

The cage lowered over the ring, and Flame unbuckled and handed the championship belt over to Sam Burnett, the referee for this match. Sam walked around the ring with the prize held high over his head, indicating it was a title match. The bell rang out, and Skywalker lunged for Flame.

Flame ducked to one side, grabbed Skywalker as he bounced off the ropes, and then slammed him face-first onto the mat. As he executed a face lock on Skywalker as he lay on the mat, Khristen slipped back into his thoughts.

Khristen's sweet face, stained with the tears he'd caused, popped into his mind. It had been the last time he'd seen her face. The hurt that he'd inflicted in the eyes he'd come to love. Shadoe surfaced as he lay in the middle of the ring. He searched for her through the cheering ringside crowd.

I have to get a grip, and fast, or I'll never come out of this match alive.

Flame relaxed his grip ever so slightly. It proved to be the moment of weakness Skywalker needed to get out of the hold.

He rolled to the edge of the mat, reached down, and came up with a baseball bat. With one swift swing, Flame fell down to his knees, reeling in agony. Pain shot through his thighs down to his feet.

Flame pulled himself up using every ounce of strength he could muster. Swinging around, he clotheslined Skywalker with such force the bat flew over the ropes, hit the links of the cage, and then landed out of the ring. Both men lay in the middle of the ring next to each other, Flame face down, and Skywalker on his back. Both gasped for air.

Sam began a ten-count as both men lay prone,

trying to gather enough strength to get up.

Instinct took over.

Flame rolled and draped an arm across Skywalker. Sam fell to the mat, sounding out the three-count. Flame felt his arm jerk up as Skywalker lifted a shoulder on the count of two.

The hold had been broken on the two-count. The match was to continue.

Each man struggled to his feet, lunged for, and dodged each other. Their bodies slammed into the cage. Flame's head snapped back, and his forehead met the unforgiving chain links. Slightly dazed, he turned into the force of a steel chair swung at him by Skywalker. His head snapped back again, and a warm, sticky substance seeped over his forehead as he fell to his knees.

Flame pushed up from his knees, lunged for, and tackled Skywalker. He straddled his downed enemy, delivering striking blows to the head with a closed fist. Anger and fury taking over his entire soul, he screamed into the face of Skywalker. Flame had resurfaced, taking control of his mind and body.

"You son of a bitch," Flame yelled.

Nose-to-nose, blood dripping, Flame slapped him once. "Get your sorry ass up and fight like a man!"

Rolling off of his opponent, he stood waiting for Skywalker to get to his feet. He wanted to beat this young punk to a pulp, to send a message to the promoters that he wasn't playing by their new rules of the game, but by the rules established in the days of ancient times. The same rules that got him where he was today...fighting to keep the championship belt around his waist. Fighting with physical power. Fighting with honor and dignity. Fighting for his life.

Uncertainty in his gaze, Skywalker faced him and dove straight ahead, flinging his own body toward the wall of chain links. Flame moved to the right at the last second, grabbing Skywalker as he bounced off the cage, driving him backward onto the mat. He hooked a leg and prayed for victory.

Skywalker struggled and pounded the mat, looking for a way to break the hold. A rake of Flame's eyes proved to be the ticket.

In agonizing pain, Flame released his hold, allowing Skywalker to roll away from him to the edge of the mat.

Staggering to his feet, Flame frantically rubbed at his eyes. His blurred vision cleared in time to see a shiny object come toward him seconds before he felt the pain of his flesh tearing.

* * * *

Khristen ran past the security she'd come to know and raced down the hallways, up the stairs, and through the curtains without anyone trying to stop her. From the top of the ramp, her full attention focused on the ring and Shadoe.

For her, it was Shadoe, not Flame, taking a beating. Shadoe was the one spilling blood, the one she ached to be holding her, loving her for all time.

She wanted to run to him now, this very minute, but her legs wouldn't move. It felt as if they were bolted to the ramp, keeping her on the outside, safe from the brutal attacks going on inside the steel cage.

Her heart sank at the brutal sound of the cage each time Shadoe's body slammed into it full-force. Helpless, she stood and watched. There wasn't a thing she could do but pray he'd somehow survive.

Her breath lodged in her chest as Skywalker connected a chair to Shadoe's head. She watched on the big screen as he rose to his knees with blood streaming over his face.

He knocked Skywalker to the mat and then sat on him. Khristen felt as if she delivered the blows to Skywalker's face. Every punch Shadoe connected caused her right arm and hand to move in unison with his. Her body moved as one with his each time he dodged Skywalker, felt the pain of his body slamming against the steel cage face-first.

White light blinded her vision. She turned from it, seeing herself on the big screen. In the next instant, she saw Shadoe turn from the force of the cage and the chair once again rip open his forehead.

"Noooo!" she screamed the sound so blood-curling, she wasn't sure where or from whom it had come, yet the sound was strangely familiar. Without a thought for herself, she ran down the ramp to the side of the ring, where Shadoe lay, bloody, his head busted wide open.

"Shadoe!"

She reached out to touch him through the chain links, tears streaming down her face at the sight of his blood on her fingertips.

"Shadoe!"

She heard herself scream again.

"Khristen." He rolled over, his blood dripping from the open wound onto her hand, recognition in his eyes.

Skywalker stood over him, sneering at her in a sickening way, licking his lips. Her stomach balked at the sight.

"The weakness," Skywalker hissed.

He grabbed Flame's head and then pulled him to his feet by a handful of hair.

"I've found your weakness, Flame," he declared.

A closed fist was delivered to Shadoe's forehead, the blow caused him to spin around and land in front of her.

"And that weakness is a woman. That woman!"

Blood splattered her face. She didn't try to stop the tears as they rolled down her cheek this time. His face was a bloody and battered mess. She felt the touch of his fingertips wipe one tear away as the last bit of Shadoe faded behind his closing eyelids.

"Shadoe!"

She tried in vain to touch his face with her fingertips through the chain. The love of her life bled all over, and there wasn't a thing she could do to stop it.

His body jerked backward at the force of Skywalker pulling him to his feet. The referee stood by as if he was a spectator watching a bar room fight.

"Let go of him!" she screamed.

Deep in her heart, she knew Skywalker would continue beating him, her plea unheard. Skywalker knocked Shadoe face-first to the mat.

"Help him, please help him," she pleaded to Sam.

She looked from the referee to Shadoe, who lay face down on the mat, not moving, and silently thanked Sam for finally keeping Skywalker back to the other side of the ring.

"Shadoe."

She wept and spilled tears on the mat, just inches from his face.

"Please wake up. Come back to me, Shadoe. You've got to wake up..." she cried.

"Khristen?" Shadoe asked, her name barely a murmur.

"Yes, yes, Shadoe, it's me."

Thank the powers of God.

She smiled with what little relief she could muster.

His eyes fluttered open, and in that instant she saw his love for her, just before they faded to the dark side, the blackness that embraced the fury living inside him. The Devil got his due, after all.

"Shadoe!"

She wanted to bring back the man who owned her heart and soul; instead she witnessed Flame take total control. All was lost.

Shadoe. Their life together. Their love.

"No!" she screamed.

Being dragged away from the cage by a couple of referees from the back, she struggled in vain to get away from them as they forced her back up the ramp.

From the big screen, she saw Flame emerge from the mat to be met by the butt of a bat jabbed into his stomach. Despair settled deep into her soul, covering her love with no hope for that light at the end of the tunnel.

One last glance at the screen proved Shadoe was truly lost to her. He battled to his feet only to be beaten to the mat once again and all for the glory of a leather belt and a piece of gold strapped around his waist.

There was no place for her here. No place for her love for Shadoe, or his for her. The ring, a mistress she couldn't hope to defeat, had burrowed deep into his soul.

CHAPTER 14

The roar of the crowd rang in her ears. Blood stained her fingers and face. Fear gripped her soul, strangling the love in her heart. Tears pooling in her eyes escaped with a blink. Khristen sat behind the steering wheel of her car trembling with fear.

"I can't do this." She sobbed in the solitude surrounding her, looking for guidance and finding none. "I can't pretend it's okay. The fighting night after night."

How could she think she belonged in his world? She may care for Shadoe in a way she thought impossible, but she could never find a place in her heart for Flame. Even if they were one and the same, there was only room for one man in her life.

The ring was the one mistress she could never fight and hope to defeat, no matter how much they'd try to fool themselves into believing otherwise, no matter how much love she saw in

Shadoe's eyes as he lay on the bloody mat. The ring would always be calling him back into her web, enticing him to make love to the sport again.

She turned the key, the purr of the engine now silent, the sound of Shadoe's cries of pain echoing loud and clear in her mind when she stepped out of the vehicle.

Surrounded by the beauty, Khristen saw only blood running from Shadoe's head as she walked through the hotel gardens. The night sky carried the carriage of destruction.

Slipping off her shoes, she dropped them in the sand. The crash of the night's ocean waves rang out like the sound of Shadoe's body hitting the steel cage.

Her life spun further and faster out of control. There wasn't anything she could do to slow the revolving downward spiral.

Although her body showed no marks, her heart was as beaten as Shadoe's body. Her spirit was bruised a hundred times more, the white light of hope put out by the darkness of despair.

The dark veil of loss enveloped her with cold, bone chilling fingers as she walked through the sand toward the beach. Khristen didn't notice the figure emerging from the patio shadows. The touch-tone sounds of a cordless phone never reached her ears.

"Emergency message for Shadoe Donovan," a deep voice whispered, "from Ric Scott. Tell him..."

* * * *

"Ugh," Flame said.

The cry didn't even begin to describe the pain that shot through him.

RINGS OF PARADISE

What the hell has he hit me with this time?

Flame fell to his knees. He spent more time laying on the mat than standing on it. This had to end, and it had to end now.

"Come on, Flame," Skywalker taunted. "You're about to be extinguished!"

Blood. Where is all the blood coming from?

Flame focused on the red-stained canvas, not yet realizing it ran down the side of his face.

"How about it, Flame? I can call the match now for loss of blood," Sam pleaded.

He looked into the kneeling referee's eyes and couldn't believe it was his flow of life spilling all over the ring.

"No, Sam... I'll finish this...one way or another," Flame said.

He struggled to his feet, anticipating the blow he was sure to come.

"Look at you, Cinderblock," Skywalker's taunt came from the other side of the ring. "You can hardly stand. Spilling your juices all over in front of a weak, crying woman...

Woman? What woman?

Flame stopped moving. Shaking the cobwebs from his head, a vision emerged of Khristen, tears on her cheeks, blood splattered on her face. His beautiful Khristen had come to his side. The touch of her fingers on his hand, the faint sound of her voice pleading for help.

The vision of Skywalker flaunting himself in front of her. The sound of his threatening voice when he spoke to Khristen brought Flame to his knees. He turned, reaching for Skywalker.

"You son of a bitch!" he screamed.

Only it wasn't Flame who cried out, it was Shadoe. The two alter egos meshed into one within the blink of an eye; no one but Shadoe was aware of it. No one but he felt the union in his soul and in his heart—two hearts and souls with love for one woman.

He moved with such quickness, Skywalker didn't know what hit him. Shadoe didn't care that he'd finally spilled some of his opponent's blood when Skywalker's head snapped back against the steel cage, busting open.

Skywalker hit the ground from his unexpected attack. Shadoe dragged him up, whipping him face first into a turnbuckle. He rolled him onto his back as he bounced off the padded corner.

Before he knew it, Sam was on the mat yelling a three-count then raising Shadoe's hand in victory. The roar of the crowd was deafening; the ring announcer's words jolted like a bolt of electric current into his head.

"And *still* your world champion, Flaaaaaame!"

The cage ascended into the rafters of the arena. Sam handed him the belt with a slap on the back. From past experience, he knew Skywalker lay in the middle of the ring trying to figure out what had just happened.

Shadoe, blood trickling down his face, jumped out of the ring. Running up the ramp, he ignored the fans at ringside. He didn't realize that what was once so precious to him lay in the middle of the battlefield he'd just left behind.

He bounded into his dressing room wanting

nothing more than to leave and find Khristen. The fact that she'd been there meant more to him than he'd ever imagined. She'd seen something he'd been trying to keep from her—the dark side of the business. At first it hadn't mattered what she did or didn't see, but for reasons too numerous to express, it did now.

"Flame." The door opened, the voice belonging to a man carrying a medical bag. "Gotta look at that head and those ribs." The man continued on in without waiting for an invitation.

The doctor dabbed away at Shadoe's forehead, cleaning the cuts and wiping away the dried blood. "Gonna need some stitches."

"So do it, then, doc."

Shadoe grimaced from the sting the antiseptic drenched sponge caused.

"You got it."

The reply came as the first suture was made followed by several others.

"Damndest match I ever saw, Flame." He continued tying up the last of the stitches. "Thought you were a goner, for sure. And the woman down there at the ring. Cryin' and fussin'...took a couple of security people and referees to pull her away from you just laying there..." the doctor said.

A ruckus at the door halted whatever else was about to come out of the doctor's mouth.

"Shadoe! Sorry, but this came during the match. He said to give it to you right away. That it was urgent."

Breathless, the young man handed a piece of folded paper over to him.

Shadoe read the words over in his mind. He bounded to his feet, grabbing his bag as he headed toward the door.

"Sorry doc, but I gotta go."

"Not until I look at those ribs, son. I gotta..."

"My ribs will heal."

Shadoe left the dressing room and the door open behind him. He had one destination in mind, his car.

My hotel. My woman. My life.

Sam Burnett came up alongside him. "Flame, you forgot this." Shadoe looked from Sam to the belt he carried. The belt he'd left behind and hadn't realized it. The very thing he'd worked so hard for all these years—the UWW Championship.

"The 'Champ' can't go without the gold." Sam draped the belt over one of Shadoe's shoulders.

"Thanks, Sam."

Turning, Shadoe headed toward the exit with nothing on his mind but the few words written on a piece of paper..."She's here. Meet me in lobby. Ric Scott."

* * * *

Screeching to a halt in front of the hotel, Shadoe bolted from the car, leaving the door open. He burst through the doors and headed for the front desk at a jog.

"Hi, Mr. Donovan," Jennifer said. "Looks like you got the worst of it tonight."

"Jennifer, has Ms. Roberts checked out yet?"

He didn't want to talk about anything, least of all the night's match.

"No, she hasn't. But the car has been back for

some time now."

"Has anyone seen her at all?"

He could only hope she was still on the island. Still in his hotel. Still somehow connected to his life.

"She's here, Donovan."

The voice, like that of a long-lost adversary, belonged to Ric Scott. Shadoe turned to face the man who could very well be the enemy.

"Scott."

"Donovan."

The two eyed each other from head to toe, both searching for answers to questions. Shadoe found his. Ric Scott was no more the enemy than Khristen. He was a person who cared deeply about a friend, not a lover.

"So, where is she?" he demanded. Shadoe took a step closer, holding in check the need to grab Scott by the shoulders.

"Out there." Scott nodded toward the dark, open garden area.

Shadoe immediately headed for the patio area, heart pounding fast in his chest with hopes and fears. The fear won. He came up short when there was no one in the gardens.

Khristen wasn't out there.

Just what the hell is Scott trying to do here?

Shadoe was in no mood to play games. He wanted to see Khristen, hold her in his arms. He turned toward Scott, his body language saying what he was afraid to say out loud.

"She's out there, Shadoe. In the night." Scott took a step closer, putting a hand on his shoulder.

"And safe. I took the liberty of having one of your employees follow her."

Relief surged through him. "Thanks." He needed to go to her, to set things right. He had to try, even if it meant losing her in the end. God help him if that happened.

"Think about it, Shadoe. You can't face her looking like you do," Scott said. "Dried blood on your face and in your hair. Not to mention looking like you came straight from the doors of hell."

"I did, and you'll never know if it was physical or emotional," Shadoe said.

The pain from the match and the brutality of the attacks took the place of the adrenaline, but not the love lodged deep in his heart—the love for a woman who had more strength than he did.

"Guess not," Scott agreed, taking a seat.

"Mr. Donovan, where would you like your gear?" asked the young man who carried Shadoe's bag and the championship belt that felt more like a ball and chain.

Shadoe looked from Peter to Scott. He knew exactly what he was going to do. It may be a little crazy, but it just might work.

"Peter, I'd like you to do something very special for me. Go to the garden and pick a couple of the best Bird of Paradise. Then..." Shadoe began.

* * * *

For her, it was over. The white light of love burned out, leaving nothing behind. There wasn't even a coal waiting for her to follow back into its warmth. She'd die old and alone, without Shadoe.

Shadoe Donovan, the one man who filled her

RINGS OF PARADISE

with burning desire and need, was lost to her now. She wanted to run as far away as she possibly could, as far as the beach would allow her to go.

She raced through the sand into the pitch-black night, seeking escape and a place to hide. She wanted to bury herself deep into the darkness and never come back.

How she ended up among the boulders, Khristen had no idea. An unexplainable force pulled her, drew her to the place where she and Shadoe had first gone, the lone boulder sitting apart from the others. The ocean gently reached out to wash the sand from the smooth surface.

Do things, places in time, repeat themselves in a person's life?

She felt so, at least at that moment she did. She felt loneliness, yet comfort on the beach. The gentle breeze of the Pacific licked across her face, chasing the horror of Shadoe's match away, bit by bit.

She ached for Shadoe's arms around her to keep her safe, secure. Fantasy was all she'd have to hold her. Shadoe was lost to her in a world she didn't understand.

She longed to have one last chance at that world, to break through his walls, to tell him she craved the warmth of his touch, to let him know her heart would always be his.

To tell him I love him.

Lost in the ocean waves, she didn't realize she was no longer alone until she saw the island boy place several Birds Of Paradise at her feet. Drawn around her in the sand was a square, placing her, the boulder, and the bright orange flowers in the middle.

Just as quietly as he'd come upon her, the boy slipped into the night's shadows.

The beat of her heart fluttered wildly against her chest like the wings of an excited caged bird. Another figure, this one taller and broader walked towards her. He advanced upon her, quietly and with purpose.

"Shadoe."

Like a fresh breath of life, his name came off her lips. Her soul cried out to touch him.

He stopped in front of her, just outside the perimeter of the sand-drawn square, championship belt in hand. He looked every bit a champion—proud, regal and more man than any woman could ever hope for.

"I've made some mistakes lately. I took for granted that you'd understand what I did and why. The magazine. Your job. Your blind trust in a man not worthy enough for it. I don't know if you'll ever be able to forgive me..."

She was about to run to him; he put his hand up to stop her words.

"This is where it all began. I don't want it to end here, or anywhere for that matter," Shadoe said. He stood in the night of paradise looking at her with so much love and passion, tears slipped from her eyes.

"Flame died tonight. All that's left is Shadoe—a man who never knew the true meaning of paradise until he found you."

His gaze never left hers, holding her fast in this place in time.

Shadoe stepped into the square; then, on one knee, picked up a single Bird of Paradise. He snapped off a bloom, placed it in her hair, and then kissed away the tears spilling down her cheeks, leaving the belt made of leather and gold lying outside the squared circle.

She smiled through her tears at the man who held her heart. "I love you, Shadoe."

ABOUT THE AUTHOR

Maxine Douglas first began writing in the early 1970s while in high school. She took every creative writing course offered at the time and focused her energy for many years after that on poetry. It wasn't until a dear friend's sister revealed she was about to become a published author that jumpstarted Maxine into getting the ball rolling; she finished her first manuscript in a month's time.

Maxine Douglas and her late husband moved to Oklahoma in 2010 from Wisconsin. Since then Maxine has rekindled her childhood love of westerns. She has four children, two granddaughters, a great granddaughter, and a gray tabby named Simon. And many friends she now considers her Oklahoma family.

One of the things Maxine has learned over the years is that you can never stop dreaming and reaching for the stars. Sooner or later you touch one and it'll bring you more happiness than you can ever imagine. Maxine feels lucky, and blessed, that over the past several years she's been able to reach out and touch the stars--and she's still reaching.

Maxine loves to hear from her readers. So, come on by and say "Hello"; Maxine would love to hear from you. You can catch her on:

Facebook ~ Instagram ~ X ~ TikTok ~ Goodreads ~ BookBub

Milton Keynes UK
Ingram Content Group UK Ltd.
UKHW030951261124
451585UK00001B/35

9 798227 564498